MISJUDGED

ANNE SCHRAFF

SADDLEBACK
PUBLISHING

URBAN UNDERGROUND

SADDLEBACK
P U B L I S H I N G
www.sdlback.com

© 2014 by Saddleback Educational Publishing

ISBN-13: 978-1-62250-764-1
ISBN-10: 1-62250-764-9
eBook: 978-1-61247-975-0

Printed in Guangzhou, China
NOR/1213/CA21302313

18 17 16 15 14   1 2 3 4 5

CHAPTER ONE

When she was a baby, the girl had a magical smile so her mother named her Mona Lisa Corsella. She was a pretty baby and a bewitching toddler, but as she grew into a teenage girl, she became painfully plain-looking. When she was thirteen, her mother was brushing her hair and she said, "Mona, you are not beautiful, but you're a nice-looking girl, and you're healthy. We've nothing to complain about."

But hearing those blunt words was very hurtful to Mona, even though she knew they were true. She'd known for a long time. But the truth was, Mona wanted to be beautiful and hot, and she never wanted it as much as now because this was her senior year at Cesar Chavez High School.

Mona stared at the really beautiful girls, like Naomi Martinez with her violet eyes and her perfect skin. Naomi had a perfect little nose and an expressive full-lipped mouth. She had a figure to match, slim but with curves in all the right places. Naomi had a boyfriend, Ernesto Sandoval, who was handsome with broad shoulders and an athlete's physique. Mona did not want to look enviously at girls like Naomi and Mira Nuñez, who dated a Chavez Cougars football star, Clay Aguirre. She did not want to stare at the pretty, lucky girls, but she couldn't help herself.

It wasn't that Mona was ugly or anything. She was five feet six inches tall, and she weighed a hundred thirty pounds. She had a nice complexion and long brown hair that she wore straight. It was just that her eyes were a tiny bit too close together, and her nose was okay, but not perfect, and her lips were a little thin, not luscious looking like Naomi's. It wasn't any one thing. It was a lot of little things, and when they all added up, Mona wasn't beautiful.

"Hi, Mona," Teri Montina, Mona's closest friend, called out as she hurried to catch up with Mona. Teri wasn't beautiful either, but she didn't seem to care that much.

"Hi, Teri," Mona said.

"Wasn't the football game on Friday a downer?" Teri said. "I sure thought we'd win. That dude from Taft, the quarterback, he's awesome. But we had a good season anyway. Chavez was in the playoffs, and that's something." Teri could always see the bright side in every situation. Mona envied her that ability.

"I was surprised Clay Aguirre didn't do better," Mona said. Everybody in the senior class knew that Aguirre was egotistical and often nasty, but he was a good linebacker. Clay was the kind of guy who wouldn't give a girl like Mona a second look.

3

"Yeah, well, it just wasn't our night," Teri said.

"Clay is so arrogant," Mona continued. "One time, I just asked him a question about a test in biology, and he sneered at me. He only talks to hot chicks."

"Not all boys are like that," Teri said cheerfully. "A lot of guys just go for a girl who's nice and friendly. She doesn't have to be all that hot."

"Dream on," Mona said a little bitterly.

"Mona, look. Two senior guys are coming this way right now. They're both on the track team, and they're in my classes too. Julio Avila and Jorge Aguilar. The other day, I watched the track team practice. Julio is like lightning, but Jorge is improving too. I bet if I said something nice to those dudes, they'd light up right away," Teri said.

Mona said nothing. Julio and Jorge were not as good-looking as dudes like Ernesto and Clay, but they were tall and well-built, and they could probably have their pick of the hot chicks at Chavez High. Boys on an athletic team always appealed to hot chicks. Mona didn't think either boy would want anything to do with Mona or Teri.

"Hey, you guys," Teri chirped. "I wanna tell you, you both looked great at track practice. I bet the Cougar track team is gonna knock the socks off the other schools."

Both Julio and Jorge stopped. Julio grinned and said, "Whoa! You hear that, Jorge? With fans like this chick, how can we miss?"

Jorge Aguilar was a lot shyer than Julio. He'd gotten in trouble a few weeks ago hanging with some gangbangers, and only Ernesto Sandoval's intervention saved him from serious trouble. He was almost bounced off the track team. But Jorge smiled too and said, "Thanks, Teri. I'm running a lot this year. I hope I can help the team."

Mona thought Julio was really handsome. He had kind of a bad-boy image. His father was little more than a bum, but if anybody made a disparaging remark about Mr. Avila, Julio turned into a bear. He really loved his father.

Mona was absolutely sure she could never get a boyfriend as cute as Julio. Too many hot chicks would be looking at the boy many said might end up in the Olympic trials because of his amazing speed on the track.

But Julio looked at Mona and said, "Somebody told me your middle name was Lisa. Mona Lisa Corsella. Is that true or were they joking with me?"

Mona felt her face turning hot. She was always keenly embarrassed by what she considered her ridiculous name. What were her parents thinking? Didn't they realize the problems they'd cause their poor daughter by sticking her with such a name? "Yeah, it's true. Crazy, huh?" she finally said, adding, "I hate it."

"Why?" Julio asked. "I think it's kinda cool. Mona Lisa is one famous chick. People have been wondering about her for

6

hundreds of years. Was she really smiling? Some dude even wrote a song about her a long time ago. How come your parents named you that? They artists or something?" He seemed really interested.

"No, my parents sell real estate," Mona said. "But my mom got this print of *Mona Lisa* when she was a kid, and she fell in love with it. When I was a baby—and this is really weird—everybody said I had a smile like Mona Lisa in the painting. Is that nuts or what? Right after I was born, in the hospital, they said I had that smile."

Julio continued looking at Mona, almost staring at her. It made her uncomfortable, and yet she was thrilled at the same time. Julio had big dark eyes, vaguely sinister, but dreamy. "Yeah, I think I can see that, yeah. Around the eyes, the mouth too. Pretty cool. Well, have a nice day, Mona Lisa." Then he walked on.

The boys walked around the corner to their class, and Teri said, "See? Weren't they nice, Mona?"

"Julio was mocking my stupid name," Mona snarled. "He was laughing at me. Couldn't you see that, Teri? He was thinking 'look at this dog with the funny name!' "

"Mona!" Teri scolded. "I don't know what's the matter with you. Both those boys were very nice, and Julio was really fascinated by your name."

"Oh, Teri, you're such a Pollyanna," Mona grumbled. "If you saw a field full of ugly stinkweeds, you'd say they were beautiful sunflowers." Mona didn't want to hurt Teri's feelings, but it was true. Sometimes Mona got so sick of Teri's relentlessly sunny disposition. A lot of the time, life could be really horrible, and if you couldn't see that, you were stupid or naïve.

"Well, *I* say we made a good impression on those boys," Teri insisted as the girls headed in different directions to their classes.

Mona knew better. Right now, those boys were laughing about the two pathetic girls who were trying to flirt with them.

They would probably spend all morning laughing about it.

Mona went into her American history class, which focused on the U.S. as a world power. An older man, Jesse Davila, was the teacher, and Mona liked him very much. He explained things so clearly, and his tests were really fair. Mona could not understand why a few of the kids in class hated Mr. Davila and made fun of him sometimes when he made a little mistake. Everybody knew Mr. Davila had a very sick wife, disabled by Parkinson's disease, and he was also helping his single daughter raise her fourteen-year-old daughter. Mona felt sorry for Mr. Davila.

The other day, Mr. Davila did something very clever, which put some of his critics to shame. With the use of videoconferencing, he allowed the students to see and talk to a woman who had once been secretary of state. It was very exciting.

Before Mr. Davila arrived to start class, Clay Aguirre was talking to his friend, Rod

Garcia. Mona disliked them both. Rod had run for senior class president, but Mona voted for Ernesto Sandoval because he seemed nicer.

"How's it going with Mira?" Rod asked Clay Aguirre.

"She's eating out of my hand, dude," Clay boasted. "She worships the ground I walk on. When I say 'jump,' she wants to know how high."

Rod laughed. "She's a really hot chick too," he said.

"Yeah," Clay said. "Would I want any other kind?"

Mona thought to herself, "Creep!"

Just then, Naomi Martinez walked into the classroom. Clay glanced at her. Everybody knew Clay used to date her, but she dumped him for Ernesto Sandoval. Mona didn't blame her. Ernesto seemed really sweet, in addition to being handsome.

Mona and Naomi had a drama class together when they were juniors, and now Naomi was friendly to Mona. She smiled and greeted her all the time.

Naomi often asked Mona to join her and her friends at lunch, but Mona never went. It made Mona feel weird because there would be Naomi and her boyfriend, and the other lovey-dovey pairs. Mona thought she'd feel like the third wheel of the wagon. It would just remind Mona that she didn't have a boyfriend and maybe never would.

Mr. Davila came in and started a lively discussion on the United States' relationship with a resurgent China. Ever since he pulled that coup bringing in the secretary of state on the screen, the class was showing him more respect, and that made him a better teacher.

"Don't you think China sees itself as the great power of the future, possibly surpassing the United States?" Mr. Davila asked the class.

Ernesto Sandoval raised his hand. "Yes, I think that's why they're pushing education so much. They want to make their education system the best in the world.

Millions of Chinese children now must learn English. Can anybody imagine if we were asking our kids to learn Chinese?" he said as the students around him laughed.

"They'll never beat out the U.S.," Clay Aguirre said, "because they're inferior."

Mr. Davila looked at Clay. There was a moment of silence in the room. "How do you mean that, Clay?" the teacher asked.

Clay Aguirre shrugged and looked around the room nervously. "Well, I mean like they're still using oxen in farming and stuff," he said.

"Yes," Mr. Davila said. "That's true in remote provinces of China. But industrially, they have made amazing strides. The United States cannot be complacent. We cannot take it for granted that our nation will always be the number-one power. Unless we all work hard and do our best, encourage innovation, develop scientists, we might slip behind."

As the class filed from the room, Clay Aguirre managed to walk alongside Naomi.

"You know, just because we lost that last game doesn't mean I'm not still considered a top football player in the high schools around here. There's a lot of buzz about me," he said.

Naomi carefully concealed the smile tugging at the corner of her mouth. "Oh … that's good, Clay."

"Yeah, a lot of guys told me I'm gonna get offers for college football scholarships. Mira is really excited. That chick hitched her wagon to a star, and the star is gonna streak across the sky," Clay said.

Naomi got the message. It was as if he were really saying, "Aren't you sorry you dumped me, girl? Don't you wish you were in Mira's shoes?"

"Wow," Naomi said. "Well, have fun, you guys." She spotted Ernesto and hurried to join him.

Mona saw Ernesto and Naomi laughing together. She felt a pang of sadness. Many times she'd imagined herself and some boy being like that. Running to be with each other, laughing together, exchanging little shows of affection. Mona was swimming in melancholy when a boy's voice came from behind her. "Where do you eat lunch, Mona Lisa?" Julio Avila asked her.

Mona turned, shocked. She couldn't believe he was really standing there. "Uh, I usually just buy something and go sit on one of the benches," Mona said. She felt weird at the way the boy was looking at her. She didn't know what to make of it. Was he still making a joke of this?

"I eat lunch with Ernesto and Abel and the gang," Julio said. "I think Naomi Martinez will be there. She usually is. I saw you and Naomi last year in that school play *Arms and the Man*. You guys seemed to know each other."

"Yes, I like Naomi," Mona said. Her heart was pounding.

"We go over there under the trees," Julio said. "I bought this huge sub. I can't eat it all, so maybe we can split it. It's got chicken, peppers, tomato, everything.

They put this great sauce on too. Man, it's good."

"Okay," Mona said, following Julio to the place under the trees where Ernesto and Naomi were already digging into their brown bags for lunch.

"Hi, Mona," Naomi said with a big smile. "Glad you're joining us. You too, Julio. Let's see what Mom packed for me here. We had a big ham, and we've been having leftovers since forever, but it was a good ham. Ham and cheese and pickles, who could ask for anything more?" Naomi looked at Mona and Julio. "What've you guys got?"

"Me and Mona are splitting a sub," Julio said.

Mona's mouth was very dry. She wasn't used to this. It didn't seem to be really happening. She felt strange. Part of her wanted to be over on her usual bench, sitting alone and watching the world go by, not feeling a part of it. But another part of her trembled with excitement. It was as if she'd stepped into another world, a bright exciting world.

Julio split the sub and handed Mona her half.

"You guys all know Mona, right?" Abel Ruiz and Bianca Marquez had arrived, and Carmen was just sitting down. Carmen Ibarra was a senior at Chavez High, but her boyfriend, Paul Morales, was older and managed an electronics store.

Everybody had seen Mona around, but they didn't know her well, except for Naomi.

"Did you know Mona's middle name is Lisa?" Julio said. "Mona Lisa Corsella."

"No," Ernesto said. "I didn't know that. Is it really, Mona?"

Mona blushed a little. She still didn't trust what was happening. Maybe Julio had lured her down here among his friends to make a big joke of her. Maybe he wanted to humiliate her in front of his friends.

It wouldn't be the first time something like that had happened to Mona. When she was a junior last year here at Chavez, a guy invited her to a school dance. He said he liked her, and Mona was really excited. Then, right after they arrived at the school gym where the dance was being held, the boy split and started hanging with another girl who he really seemed to like. Mona stood on the sidelines all evening wanting to die. She kept catching glimpses of the boy laughing at her. Later on, she found out he had made a bet with his friends that he could ask a girl to the dance and then ditch her and leave her swinging in the wind.

"Yes," Mona managed to say. "Mona Lisa is my full name."

"That's a beautiful name," Naomi said. "Remember, Mona, you told me last year that your parents named you for the lady in the famous painting."

"Yeah," Ernesto said, "da Vinci painted *Mona Lisa*. I guess she's one of the most fascinating ladies in the art world. My grandfather has all the records that Nat King Cole made—if you guys heard of him—anyway, he sang that song about Mona Lisa, and it was cool."

Mona felt ill at ease, but she had to admit the sub sandwich was good. She kept waiting for the other shoe to drop and for everybody to start laughing at her.

Then Naomi said, "You guys, I ran into Clay Aguirre, and he's bragging about being a great football star. What an ego. Did you hear him, Mona?"

Suddenly, a dark look crossed Julio's face. "That's a real mean dude. He really dissed my pop, and I almost did him serious harm." He turned to Mona. "My pop, he hasn't had a good life, but I'm gonna make him proud with my running. I love the guy. He's always been there for me." Julio was looking right into Mona's eyes, and in spite of herself, her heart leaped.

CHAPTER TWO

Mona Lisa lived with her parents in a roomy condo on Cardinal Street. Two years ago, Mona's older brother joined the Marines. Six months ago, her younger brother, Peter, joined up too. Now only Mona and her parents lived in the condo. Xavier and Martha Corsella were both real estate agents, and for a long time, they were doing very well. When the real estate market collapsed, all that changed. They still occasionally closed deals, but money was tight. Mona's parents often said that it was good that her brothers had joined the military because affording college would have been difficult.

Mona had a part-time job at the frozen

yogurt shop, and she'd always hoped that she'd have a used car of her own by the time she was a senior. But now that her parents needed some of her salary to pay the bills, that was out of the question. Mona took the bus to and from school or walked.

"I'm home," Mona announced, coming in the front door. The minute anyone stepped into their living room, they would see the photographs of the two Marines in their uniforms. Mom and Dad were very proud of them. Then there were school photos of Mona, but Mona hated the way they came out.

Usually, Mona was in a blah mood when she got home, but today she was a little happy. Eating lunch with Julio and his friends lifted her spirits. She was sure it was only her fevered imagination, but Julio seemed to like her.

"Well, Mona," Mom said, "you seem chipper today. Did you get a good grade on a test or something?"

"Uh, yeah, I got an A in math," Mona

said. But that had nothing to do with her mood. Mona was a very good student, and she'd come to expect good grades.

"That's good," Mom said.

Mona would never share what happened at lunch with her mother. At this point, Mona thought it was just a fluke anyway, and she didn't want to appear like a desperate fool. She knew it was a source of worry to her mother that she never seemed to have a boyfriend. When Mona went to the junior prom last year, she suffered the ultimate indignity of being escorted by her brother, Peter. He got all the attention too, with the girls flocking around him. Mona's brothers were good-looking with dark eyes and dark hair just like Mona. But the facial expressions that looked good on them did not look as good on her.

Mona was pretty sure nothing would come of her brief contact with Julio Avila, so she didn't want to involve her mother.

Her dad came into the front room then. Xavier Corsella looked sad as usual. He

21

worked so hard trying to sell his listings, but a month could go by without a single commission. "I wish this market would turn around," he often said. "I thought I had a couple interested in a house on Bluebird Street, but when they went for a loan, they didn't qualify."

"That's too bad," Mom said.

Mona got a text message after she went to her room. The only person from school who texted her was Teri, but the message wasn't from her this time.

"Hey, Mona, remember me?" Julio Avila wrote. "I'm running in the division championships in Balboa Park tomorrow. It's a three-mile run. Come and watch, and then we'll go for something to eat. K? Julio."

Mona was stunned. When her mother passed her room, she saw the girl sitting there with a strange look on her face. "What's the matter, honey?" she asked.

"Oh … nothing … a friend of mine is running in Balboa Park tomorrow, and maybe I'll go watch," Mona said.

"That's nice," Mom said. She assumed the friend was a girl.

Mona texted Julio back, "I'll be there. Bet you'll win, Mona."

Then Mona called Teri. "Oh, Teri, you won't believe this, but Julio Avila texted me to come watch him run in Balboa Park tomorrow."

"Didn't I tell you, girl?" Teri cried. "You just need to be a little friendly and the boys will come like puppies. Guys are very simple creatures. Mom keeps telling me that. They're more afraid of us than we are of them."

"Oh, Teri, I was just shocked," Mona said. "Julio is such a jock. He's the top runner on the Cougars track team, and the girls all look at him. There must be lots of cute girls flocking around him. Why would he be interested in me?"

"Mona, don't put yourself down. You got a lot more going on for you than you think. Go and cheer your head off tomorrow, girl," Teri said.

At dinner, even Dad noticed that there was something different about Mona. "You've got a glow about you, Mona," he said.

"I really had a nice day at school," Mona said.

"She got an A in math," Mom said.

"Good for you, Mona," Dad said. "But you're always getting good grades. You sure there isn't something else going on?" Dad smiled a little. "After all, you're a lovely young lady, and one of these days a special boy is going to notice that."

Mom had told Mona that she wasn't beautiful, and that had hurt her very much. But Dad had never said that. Dad was always telling Mona how cute she was, and even though Mona didn't believe it, she was grateful to her father for saying it.

"Well," Mona said, breaking down, "some senior boy is being real nice to me. I mean, no big thing, but he invited me to have lunch with him today—with him and his friends."

24

Dad winked. "I knew it! There's a special glow on a girl's face when a boy is paying her special attention. Who is the boy?"

"Oh, he's a friend of Ernesto Sandoval," Mona said.

A big smile came to Mom's face. "Ernesto Sandoval—the senior class president. He's a wonderful boy. He comes from an excellent family. You couldn't hang out with a better group of kids than Ernesto and his friends," she said.

"Yeah," Dad chimed in. "I play basketball with Ernesto's dad, Luis. He's a great guy."

"Did you say who the boy who was nice to you was, Mona?" Mom finally realized that Mona had omitted that information. Mona was a little nervous about mentioning Julio Avila. Everybody knew that Julio's father lived on the street for a while. Now he and his son lived in a small trailer in a run-down park. They survived on Mr. Avila's disability check from Social Security and on Julio's pay as a part-time bag boy in the supermarket.

Sometimes, Mr. Avila stood on Washington Street and asked for spare change. He smoked and sometimes drank too much. He looked much older than his late forties, with a deeply lined face and sunken eyes. Mona knew that her parents put great store in good families, and she feared they wouldn't be pleased that her new friend was the son of Mr. Avila.

Mona did something she rarely did, but she thought she had no choice. "Oh, you guys know Abel Ruiz," she said. She didn't come right out and say the boy was Abel Ruiz, but she left that distinct impression.

"Oh," Mom said with enthusiasm. "He's a fine boy. I talk to his mother all the time. Their son, Tomás, he's in college, and he's almost a genius from what his mother says."

Mona concentrated on her salad. She was ashamed of what she had done, deceiving her parents. "There's no big deal about it. We're just sorta friends," she said.

"Well, you never can tell," Dad said

happily. "Great oaks from little acorns grow."

The Corsellas laughed. The atmosphere around the dinner table improved sharply. Although the real estate market was still slow, their little ugly duckling was getting some attention. That was especially important to Mom. Mona once overheard her talking on the phone to her own mother. "Mona has no social life. I'm really sick about it. When I was her age, I had two boyfriends, and Mona has never even been on a real date. She's a senior in high school, for heaven's sake! I hope she's not turning out like Corinne. That would just break my heart. Corinne has had such a dreadful life."

Corinne was Mom's older sister, now in her forties. She had never married, and she now lived in New Orleans and owned a mask shop in the French Quarter. Mona's mother always described her as a bitter, lonely middle-aged woman who had never been asked to be somebody's wife. A few times, Aunt Corinne had come to visit Mona and her family, and she seemed to Mona to be a delightful, happy vagabond. She had traveled all over the world, from the Great Wall of China to a safari in Africa. She had seen the pyramids of Egypt and ridden on the Siberian Railroad in Russia. Sometimes, when Mona was very depressed, she thought she'd like to go live with Aunt Corinne in New Orleans.

But, unlike Aunt Corinne, Mona really *did* want a boyfriend and eventually a family. She wanted a boyfriend she could snuggle with like Naomi snuggled with Ernesto. When she saw Ernesto sneak a kiss from Naomi, she ached with envy.

"Maybe Julio would just be a good friend," Mona thought. But the idea that he was even mildly interested in her was thrilling. Just the idea of hanging out with Julio and his friends made Mona want to dance in her bedroom.

Coach Muñoz was in Balboa Park with the Cougars of the Cesar Chavez High track team early in the morning. Teri had her own car, and she drove Mona down to Balboa Park. Otherwise, Mona would have taken the bus. Teri had an old car, but to Mona it was a treasure. Mona already had her driver's license, and her father let her drive the family car once in a while, but that wasn't the same as having her own wheels like Teri had.

Ernesto Sandoval, Julio Avila, Jorge Aguilar, and the other boys were lining up for the run. Eddie Gonzales and Rod Garcia were a little late, and Coach Muñoz glared at them.

"Hi, Mona Lisa," Julio yelled when he spotted Mona behind the ropes.

"Hi, Julio," Mona shouted back.

Naomi walked up to Mona and Teri. "Don't the guys look amazing?" she said, giggling.

"Yeah," Mona said.

Naomi smiled at Mona and said, "Julio said you were pretty. He told Ernesto yesterday afternoon."

Mona had never heard anything like that about herself before. "You sure?" she gasped.

"Yeah," Naomi said, laughing. "You've got a fabulous smile, Mona."

Mona felt her skin turn warm. She thought Naomi was just trying to be nice. "You sure Julio was talking about me, Naomi?" she asked.

Naomi gave Mona a playful push. "Is there another Mona Lisa Corsella at Chavez?" she asked.

"Coach Muñoz looks really nervous," Teri said. "What a boost it would be for the Cougars to get the team title."

Ernesto was six foot one now, and Rod Garcia was six foot two. Rod had a longer stride, and he desperately wanted to beat Ernesto to get a little bit even for Ernesto beating him out of the senior class presidency. Julio Avila was six foot two also, and he had an amazing stride. He had strong motivation too.

Mr. Avila stood there alone behind the

ropes, his skinny body in a shabby over-coat. There was nothing about him that didn't look old and worn out, except for his bright black eyes that came alive when he looked at his son. Everything in the man's life had gone sour—his marriage, his many jobs, his health—and Julio was his only joy, his only reason for living.

The race was on, and family and friends along the route cheered for their favorites. Naomi Martinez was yelling for Ernesto, as were Ernesto's parents and little sisters.

The Cougars from Chavez High were never competitive in track until last year. Coach Muñoz was nearing the end of his career as a coach, and he had little to cele-brate until Ernesto, Julio, and Rod came along. Now, finally, the Cougars had a chance to beat everybody else in the county. They were even hotter this year than last.

Mona was watching Julio when she heard another girl scream, "Go, Julio!" Mona turned her head sharply to see a tall, pretty girl in a purple hoodie. She was really

31

cute. It was Amanda Carrillo who was also in Mr. Davila's American history class. Amanda was a very popular girl, and her parents were doing well. She was always one of the first girls at Chavez to wear the newest fashions. Resentment boiled up inside Mona's heart. Why was Amanda screaming for Julio? She had plenty of guys who liked her.

Mona felt like a fool then. What was she being jealous for? She was fighting for a relationship that probably didn't even exist. Just because Julio showed her a little attention, she was freaking out. Maybe, Mona thought with horror, Amanda was really Julio's girlfriend, and they'd been together for a long time. Maybe he just felt sorry for Mona. Maybe it was nothing but that.

Mona's mind was spinning as fast as the runners' legs. Didn't Julio say that she and he would go someplace to eat after the race? That sounded almost like a date. Didn't it? Maybe Julio would take a bunch of kids to lunch, maybe even including his *real* girlfriend, Amanda. Mona was feeling like a fool with every minute. She was picturing them all sitting in a restaurant with Amanda running her fingers through Julio's hair like Naomi did with Ernesto.

Loud screams of excitement rose from the fans behind the ropes as a tall, dark-haired boy pulled out in front late in the race.

"Ju-li-o, Ju-li-o," the chants rose in volume.

Julio had run the three-mile course in fifteen minutes and ten seconds. He had won the race for Chavez High. Even better from Coach Muñoz's standpoint, Rod Garcia came in second, and Ernesto Sandoval came in third, giving the team title to the Chavez Cougars.

Julio Avila went over to the ropes where his father stood. Tears streamed down the man's cheeks, running like rivers down his tired face. Julio hugged his father and said, "This is nothing, Pop. Wait'll I qualify for the Olympics. Wait'll you see them putting that gold medal around my neck, with them playing our national anthem."

Then Julio turned, his gaze scanning the people behind the ropes. Amanda was about ten feet from Mona. Mona knew Julio would go to her, and they'd go off together. He had probably forgotten all about Mona.

Then Julio looked at Mona and a smile broke out on his face. He came over and said, "Hey, Mona Lisa, you brought me luck. Give me ten minutes to clean up, and I'll meet you by my truck. The green monster over there. It's so old I think Henry Ford himself drove it at the turn of the century. If you don't mind riding in a rust bucket, we'll be off and running in a few."

Mona could only nod and babble. "You were awesome," she gasped. "I've never seen anyone run so fast in my life."

Mona rushed to tell Teri she wouldn't need a ride home. "He's taking me to eat somewhere, Teri," Mona said. She was trembling. She couldn't believe this was actually happening.

"Girl, get a grip." Teri laughed. "He's gonna think you're a nutcase."

Teri and Mona high-fived each other, and Teri went to join some other friends.

Julio had not even looked at Amanda, Mona told herself. She was right there, only about ten feet away, and Julio didn't even look at her!

"He came to me," Mona kept thinking to herself, over and over.

Mona barely heard the loud voices of the two boys nearby, but one of them finally got so loud that she looked.

"I beat you, Sandoval," Rod Garcia was crowing. "I beat you. And next time, I'll beat Avila too. I've never run so fast. Today was my best time ever. I'm gonna be the fastest runner on the Cougars, man. I'll be going to the cross-country state championships before you or Avila."

"Dream on, dude," Ernesto Sandoval said. "Nobody can stop Julio. He's got destiny on his side. One day, you and me will be sitting in our houses looking at the

Olympics on TV, and we'll see the dude get his gold. He's lightning, man."

"Sometimes you can trap lightning in a bottle, dude," Rod said.

"No way, dude. You'll be eating that homie's dust every time you chase him in a race. Get used to it," Ernesto quipped.

Mona was standing alongside a very ugly green truck as Julio walked up. There were so many rust spots on the truck that it looked almost yellow. "Let's go, babe," Julio said, opening the passenger side of the cab.

Mona felt light-headed. He had called her "babe." The sound of it was the sweetest music on earth. She turned the word over and over in her mind, savoring it.

CHAPTER THREE

Y ou really are a good runner," Mona said as the truck sprang into motion. "I bet you love to run."

"Yeah," Julio said. "I don't like playing football or soccer or baseball. Running is just me against my own best. I like that. Hey, how do you feel about going to a barbeque restaurant? My pop has a friend who runs the place. They got baby back ribs that are super."

"Sounds good," Mona said.

"Yeah, Pop used to be in the merchant marine. He met a lot of different people. He made a lot of buddies. Most of them didn't have much more luck than he did. But this dude finally got enough money together to open a little hole-in-the-wall eatery," Julio said. "I like to throw business his way."

"I saw your father during the race, Julio," Mona said. "He seemed so excited. His eyes just sparkled when he saw you leading the pack."

Julio laughed. "Pop loves to watch me run. He's got pictures of me running all over the place." Julio glanced over at Mona, his smile fading, and a more serious look coming to his face. "It's always been just Pop and me. Mom's been gone a long time. Just him and me. I remember being a little kid when times were bad, and we'd have to find a place to sleep. Anyplace."

"That must have been hard," Mona said.

"Yeah, but to a kid, you don't know any better. I thought all kids were sneaking around at night with their dads looking for a place to crash. One time, we came to this house with a For Sale sign on it. Pop goes, 'Maybe it's not locked.' And the back door was open. That was a good gig for us. We had a nice bathroom and even beds to sleep in. It was great until some dude from the bank showed up. The joint was in foreclosure. Man, we got out of there fast. I guess we were trespassing. You shoulda seen us run. Pop can't move so well anymore. He's got arthritis in his legs. But that day, man, we were both going at Olympic speed."

Mona tried to imagine what it would be like not to have her nice bedroom with the posters on the walls and a bathroom to herself. She didn't think she'd see it as an adventure. But then Julio didn't know any better.

"I work at the supermarket, Mona. You got a job?" Julio asked.

"Yeah, I work part time at the yogurt shop," Mona said. "I'd been saving for a car. I wanted a car by now, but my parents sell real estate and nothing has been moving, so I help pay some of the bills." The moment Mona said that, she regretted it. Even with the bad real estate market, the Corsellas were a lot better off than Julio and his father.

"I hear you," Julio said. "I gotta kick in most of my pay too. Pop gets a small disability check, but it's not enough to keep us going. They promoted me from box boy to checker, though, so I'm getting a raise."

They went inside the tiny restaurant decorated with folk art. A friendly looking man took their order, and the baby back ribs with a spicy sauce quickly arrived. Ribs were often tough, but here the meat was falling off the bone.

"You know," Julio explained, "they cook it real slow, and that's what makes it tender. Abel Ruiz and I came here with my pop one day, and he talked to the chef. Abel is gonna be a chef, you know. You know him, don't you?"

"Yeah, he's nice. Wow, Julio, when my mom makes ribs they are so tough … I can't believe how delicious this is," Mona said.

"Spread the word, babe. My buddy here needs business," Julio said. "Speaking of Abel Ruiz," Julio continued. "He and Ernesto Sandoval are my best homies.

When that creep Aguirre was dissing Pop and trying to make trouble for him over some poor homeless dude who was offed in the ravine, I almost killed Aguirre. He was hinting that my pop had something to do with that murder, and I just went at him. If it hadn't been for Ernie and Abel stopping me, I'd probably be doing fifteen to life in the slammer right now."

Mona was horrified, but she tried not to show it. "Friends are real important," she said, hoping that Julio had been exaggerating the incident.

"Yeah," Julio said. "Friends got your back."

As they drove home, Julio said, "You know, I remember you when we were sophomores. You wore your hair different then, kind of curly."

"Yeah, I tried that," Mona said. "Now I just let it go straight and brush it."

"I like that," Julio said. "It's like a brown shiny curtain that frames your face. Pretty. I think long straight hair is cool. You were shy when you were a sophomore. I guess I was too, around chicks anyway."

"I still am kinda shy," Mona confessed.

"Once or twice when we were juniors, I smiled at you, but you blushed and turned your head," Julio said.

"Sounds like me," Mona admitted.

"You know," Julio said, "we wouldn't be together now if it weren't for your friend, Teri, talking to me and Jorge when we came walking along. I'd thought about asking you out before, but girls don't always take to me. But you were pretty easy to talk to. And that cool name you got. That really got under my skin. There's a mystery to the *Mona Lisa*, you know. Nobody really knows who she was, who da Vinci used as a model. There's a mystery about the smile too. I look at you, and you got that same cute smile, and I'm trying to figure out what it means. I mean, do you like me or are you thinking, 'What a jerk!'?"

Mona turned numb. "Uh … I like you, Julio, a lot," she said, but that wasn't the entire truth. The truth was that she was strongly attracted to the boy, and yet she was a little scared of him too. He came from a place she'd never been, a dark sort of place where anger flared and violence was one punch away.

Mona had often glanced at homeless men, people like Julio's father. She always felt sorry for them, but at the same time she felt sure they were not like her or her family. They were much, much different. They were from a different world. But Julio was also from that world.

"I like you too, Mona," Julio said. "Today was good for me. Was it good for you too?"

"Yeah," Mona said.

Julio pulled his truck to the curb in front of Mona's condo, and she got out. On her way up the walk, she turned to wave at Julio, and he waved back. Then he drove away.

Nobody was home when Mona walked inside the condo. Her parents were out showing real estate. Mona hoped they'd have good news when they got home.

On the far wall of the living room hung Mom's print of *Mona Lisa*. Mona had often glanced at it, but now she stopped and really stared at the lady in the painting. She had long, dark hair like Mona. She had brown eyes, not spaced like Mona's were, but close. Her nose seemed a bit longer than Mona's. Mona thought her own nose was prettier. But the mouth was startling. The soft upper lips and the fuller bottom lips. Mona always felt a little strange to have been named for the lady in the painting.

When Mona saw Ernesto at the vending machine on Monday, she walked over. He turned and smiled. "The apples look so good. I like the crunchy ones," he said.

"Ernie, have you got a minute?" Mona asked.

"Sure. I'll get my apple, and we'll go over and sit on the bench. You want an apple too?" Ernesto said.

"No," Mona said, eager to talk to him. Mona didn't know Ernesto Sandoval real well, but everybody said he was really nice and friendly, even though he was the big-shot senior class president and all. He was a good athlete too. He finished third in that three-mile run.

"Uh, Ernie, I sorta like Julio Avila, and I went to see him run, and then we had lunch at a little restaurant, and I think maybe he likes me a little bit. But, you know, he told me something that scared me. He said he got really mad at Clay Aguirre one time. He said he woulda killed him maybe if you and Abel Ruiz hadn't stopped him. That sort of scared me. Did it really happen like that?" Mona blurted out.

"Well, the thing is, Mona, Clay Aguirre can be really awful. I mean, that dude knows just what buttons to push. He knew how much Julio loves his father, and yet he was out there spreading rumors that Mr. Avila killed this man. It was a totally crazy lie, but Clay was making the most of it just

45

to yank Julio's chain. Yeah, Julio lost it, and Abel and I cooled him down, but he wouldn't have killed anybody. He's got a hot temper, but he'd never hurt somebody," Ernesto said.

Mona breathed a sigh of relief. "That makes me feel better, Ernie. Thanks so much. I haven't had a lot of boyfriends … I mean, I haven't really had any, and it was so fun being with Julio."

Ernesto smiled. "Julio is a good guy. He's one of my favorite homies. He's put himself on the line for me and the other guys. He's got our backs and we got his," Ernesto said.

"I guess Julio and his father are really poor, huh?" Mona asked.

"Yeah, that's true. The dad, he almost broke his back when he was in the merchant marine, and he gets a disability check, but it's not much. They live in a trailer park at the end of Oriole. But Julio and his dad do okay," Ernesto said.

"Yeah," Mona said. "My parents were

doing really good selling real estate until the bust. They used to think if you're really down and out, it's your own fault. That you're lazy. But now they lost money in their 401(k), and they're not flying so high."

Ernesto nodded. "When everything is going your way, it's easy to think you're pretty smart, and you earned the good life by doing everything right. They figure what happens to you is in your own hands, but not always. The economy turns around and bites you. You get sick. Stuff happens. You can't judge," he said.

"My brothers, Jimmy and Peter, they're both in the Marines," Mona said. "They've always been good guys. My parents are so proud of them."

"They should be," Ernesto said.

When Mona got home from school that day, her mother was in a very bad mood. No real estate deals had been made over the weekend. What was worse, Mona's mother had run into Abel Ruiz's mother in the beauty shop.

"I made a fool of myself thanks to you lying to me, young lady," Mona's mother said crossly. "The other day at dinner, you said you were dating Abel Ruiz, and when I told his mother how happy I was about that, she looked at me as if I had just stepped out of a UFO. Abel is not dating *any* girl seriously, and when he does go out, it's with somebody named Bianca. I was mortified."

"I never said I was going out with him," Mona said, knowing she had implied it. "I just said I was friends with a boy in class, and he was close to Ernesto Sandoval and Abel Ruiz. I'm not dating anybody, Mom."

"Who is this mysterious boy?" Mrs. Corsella demanded.

"I don't even know his name," Mona lied. "He's in one of my classes, and he said some nice things to me, that's all. Can we just change the subject, Mom? It doesn't mean anything. Can we just drop it?" Mona was seething with anger.

Martha Corsella looked at her daughter with a mixture of annoyance and pity. "All right, Mona. There's no need to get angry about it. I know you feel sensitive about not having a boyfriend. I really do understand—"

"No, Mom, you do not understand. You've never understood anything about me," Mona snapped. She turned sharply, going to her room and slamming the door behind her.

Mona heard her mother on the phone to Grandma then. Mom thought Mona was safely in her room and wouldn't overhear anything, even though Mom talked loud because her mother was a little bit deaf.

Mona turned off her computer, opened the door, and listened.

"Mom, I'm really worried about Mona. She has no social life at all, and now she's begun to make things up about having boyfriends. She made a big deal about some boy who was supposedly interested in her, and it turned out he hardly knew who she was. When I asked her about it, she just flew into a rage. She's so desperate for a boyfriend that she's begun to live in a fantasy world. Oh, Mom, I'm seeing more of Corinne in her every day. I just don't know what to do."

There was silence then as Mona's mother listened to what Grandma had to say. Then, finally, she said, "Yes, I could do that. Yes, of course. Mrs. Oriana has a son in the senior class—Louis. I'm sure if his mother asked him, he'd be willing to take Mona out. It wouldn't be any commitment or anything, of course. Just for a boy to ask her out would mean so much to the poor child."

Mona's hands gathered into fists. She was so angry she thought she could punch a hole in the bedroom wall. How dare her mother talk about her like that.

Mona knew Louis Oriana very well. He was a creepy boy who hung out with Clay Aguirre and Rod Garcia, the guy who lost the senior class presidency to Ernesto

Sandoval. Louis was always making nasty remarks about girls. He'd laugh and say this one was a pig because she weighed a little too much, and that one was ugly. Then Clay and Rod would double over laughing. Mona always thought that trio was the most disgusting group of boys at Chavez High, and to think her mother was plotting to foist Louis Oriana on her!

Mona felt like rushing into the front room and telling her mother she had heard the whole conversation that she had with Grandma. Mom should just mind her own business because Mona *did* have a boyfriend right now, who was wonderful and cool. It happened to be none of her mother's business who he was.

But Mona did not have the courage to do that. She sat in her room, boiling and thinking about what she would like to say to her mother if she were brave enough.

Mona turned her computer back on and tried to focus on a project she was doing for Mr. Davila in American history. She got nowhere. All she could do was burn with rage against her mother and melt with joy at the thought that tomorrow she would see Julio at school, and they'd probably eat lunch together under the eucalyptus trees with Ernesto and Naomi and the gang.

In the morning, as she arrived at school, Mona saw Louis Oriana sitting in the passenger seat of a brand new car. Clay Aguirre was at the wheel. Clay had received the insanely expensive car from his parents, and he let his close friends ride in it.

Mona longed so much for a car—any car—even a total junker, and here was Clay flaunting his new ride. Clay and Louis came walking toward Mona. They were both laughing. Mona could imagine what they said about her on the way to school. She was boiling mad, but she made up her mind to be cool on the outside.

CHAPTER FOUR

Louis was a tall, skinny boy with a very short haircut. Mona thought he looked like some kind of nasty animal, perhaps a weasel.

"Hi, Mona," Louis said. "You're in my history class, aren't you?"

"Hi," Mona said. "Yeah. Mr. Davila's class."

"Yeah, that old dude. He's got dementia, you know. I'm sure you hate him as much as the rest of us do, but he's got tenure. One of these days, the district will wake up and stop that nonsense," Louis said.

"I like Mr. Davila," Mona said, trembling with rage. "I think he's one of the best teachers I've ever had."

Louis looked miffed, but he smiled and said, "I've been looking at you, Mona, and you seem really nice. Maybe after school we could go for pizza?"

"I hate pizza," Mona said. "It gives me heartburn." The truth was, Mona loved pizza, and she never got heartburn.

"Oh," Louis said, "well, we could get something else, then—maybe—"

"Thanks, but I'm busy after school," Mona snapped. She turned on her heel and stomped off without cracking a smile. Louis Oriana stood there, dumbfounded.

Mona thought to herself, "Surprised, huh, creep? I'd never be desperate enough for somebody like you!"

At lunchtime, Julio showed up to ask Mona to join him and his friends under the eucalyptus trees. Mona wondered if Abel would show up and if his mother had said anything. She hoped not. But, as soon as Mona sat down with Julio, Abel came along. Bianca Marquez was not with him.

"No Bianca again?" Ernesto asked.

Bianca had been missing for a few days now.

"We had a fight," Abel said.

"Oh no," Naomi said, "a little one or a major one?"

"A major one," Abel said sourly. "I've been irked with her for weeks, and it all came to a head three days ago. I just blew up at her." Abel glanced at Naomi then. "You're about the same height as Bianca. How much do you weigh, Naomi?"

"One seventeen," Naomi said.

"Yeah and you look great," Abel said. He turned to Mona, "How about you? You're about five four, right?"

"I'm five six. I weigh one thirty," Mona said.

"Yeah, and you look really good," Abel cried triumphantly. "Look at these girls here. They weigh a normal weight, and they look wonderful. Bianca, she won't eat anything but lettuce. I took her out, and she sat there drinking diet soda. I asked her what she weighed, but she wouldn't tell me. She looks haggard. I don't think she weighs more than a hundred pounds, if that. She's got this crazy mother who thinks girls should look like skeletons. She says guys like to hug bags of bones and hear them rattle."

"Maybe she's got anorexia, Abel," Naomi said. "I heard that girls actually die from it."

"You'd think her mom would call a doctor," Julio said.

"I called Mrs. Marquez yesterday," Abel said. "She goes, 'Oh, Bianca is just like me. Being slim is actually very healthy. The big problem in our society is obesity.' I don't even want to be with her anymore, you guys. If she's gonna be killing herself, I don't want to be around to see it. I told her that, and she cried and stuff, but I can't help it."

Carmen Ibarra, who was eating lunch with the gang, said, "You can't just let it go, Abel. It's a dangerous mental health issue. I heard the suicide rate is pretty high for girls with anorexia. Is she in school today?"

"Yeah," Naomi said, "I saw her in my morning class, but she really looked awful."

"She was in AP History," Ernesto said, "but she seemed groggy. I asked her if something was wrong. I told her she needed to see a doctor."

"She left early," Julio said. "I saw her walking on Washington away from school."

Abel took out his cell phone and called Bianca. After a few minutes, he frowned and shook his head. "She's not picking it up," he said. The frustration grew on Abel's face. "I'm calling her house."

"Yeah, Mrs. Marquez," Abel said. "We're all worried about Bianca. She's not picking up her phone. She seemed awful weak this morning. She left school early. Did she get home okay? … What? … Alone? When does she usually get home when she walks? … No, I'm not being nosy, ma'am. I'm worried. I'm worried about your daughter. I'm real surprised that you're not worried." Abel angrily hit the End button. He glared at his friends, shaking with rage. "She doesn't have a clue. What an idiot! Her kid is out there walking home alone, so weak she's wobbly, and her mother isn't concerned."

After school, Abel tried to call Bianca again. She still wasn't picking up her phone. "I'm going to see if Bianca is in the park," he declared to his friends.

"We'll follow you," Ernesto said. "Naomi and Carmen are coming with me. It's not a big park, but we can cover it quicker if there are more of us."

Julio looked at Mona. "Want to come along? I'll be looking for the girl too."

"Sure," Mona said. She always got home from school at the exact same time. Her mother would worry if she were late. Mona picked up her cell phone and called home. "Mom, I'm gonna be late. There's a meeting at school," she said.

"A meeting?" Mrs. Corsella questioned. "What meeting? You didn't say anything about a meeting this morning."

"It just came up, Mom. I gotta go," Mona said. Mona had never done anything like this before. She always lived in her own safe little world occupied by her parents and her brothers. She was never part of a group like this before. She was amazed how quickly they mobilized to search for a friend who might be in trouble. It was like an unspoken code. Somebody was in trouble, and they all had her back.

Abel led the way in his car, followed by Ernesto in the Volvo and Julio in his creaky green truck. They arrived at the park, and the six seniors piled out of their vehicles. Everybody was familiar with the park, the way the woodsy trails intersected, the ravines, the lake.

Mona hurried along with Julio. He seemed to know the park even better than any of the rest. He turned and said to Mona, "Pop and I spent a lot of nights here."

"Oh, that's fun to go camping in the park and stuff," Mona said. "My parents and brothers and I would—"

"No," Julio said, "we weren't on a camping trip. We *lived* here. When we couldn't get a place, we came down here with our bedrolls and sacked out with the other bums. We'd stay for weeks, until the cops came."

Mona said nothing.

The trail got narrow and steep as they went downhill toward a ravine. Julio grasped Mona's hand firmly. "Watch your step. The rains we just had washed out this trail pretty bad." Then suddenly, Julio's voice stopped. He pulled out his cell phone. "Ernesto, call Abel, we're above the ravine at the overlook. You know where that … Yeah. I see something."

Mona turned cold. She saw it too. Amid the brush below was something bright red.

Bianca Marquez wore a red pullover sweater that morning.

Mona's heart was pounding. She didn't know Bianca Marquez, except just to see the very slender girl going to classes. She seemed even more shy than Mona. They had never even had a real conversation though they sometimes smiled and waved at each other.

"Her backpack," Julio said. "It fell right here. It's got a butterfly logo." Julio picked up the muddy backpack.

"Oh my God," Mona said, her throat tightening.

Ernesto, Abel, Naomi, and Carmen came running. They picked their way down the trail. Abel looked pale. Mona glanced at the boy. He was shaking. His gaze was fixed like a laser on the red object in the brush below.

"I think it's her," Abel said in a strangled voice.

Mona started to cry. She didn't know the girl. Until this moment, she had never given Bianca Marquez a second thought. But still she started to cry.

Bianca Marquez was lying in a small creek at the bottom of the ravine. She was lying on her side as if she were sleeping. She had apparently dropped her backpack

61

and fallen. Then, at the bottom, she curled up in a fetal position and just lay there.

The six seniors reached her, but Abel was first. He knelt down at the girl's side and yelled, "Call nine-one-one!" As Ernesto was dialing 911, Abel called the Marquez home. "We found Bianca in a ravine in Washington Park … she's alive but she's in bad shape. We've called nine-one-one," he said.

"What have you done to my daughter?" Mrs. Marquez screamed. "What did you do?"

"What didn't you do, lady?" Abel said, disconnecting the call.

A fire engine, ambulance, and police car came with their sirens screaming. Mona shook with the emotion of the moment as Abel knelt by the motionless girl and spoke soft words no one could hear. A late-model sedan pulled up at the top of the hill, parking near a police cruiser. A pretty, thin woman, assisted by a police officer, rushed down the trail toward the ravine. "My baby! My baby!" she cried as the paramedics worked on Bianca.

CHAPTER FOUR

Police officers came over to talk to them. Abel talked the most. "She's kinda my girlfriend," he said. "And lately, she's been getting skinnier and skinnier, and I tried to get her to see a doctor. I called her mother, but she said nothing was wrong. I was getting scared. Today, she acted real weird and left school early, and I called her mother and she said Bianca walks by herself in the park sometimes. Me and my friends found out she wasn't home yet at like four o'clock, and so we all came to look for her."

"And then we spotted her down there," Julio said. "She musta dropped her backpack and sorta slid down the hill."

"She's a good girl," Mrs. Marquez was sobbing. "She doesn't use drugs or drink. I can't understand what happened."

Bianca was on a gurney with an oxygen mask over her face as they took her to the ambulance. Her mother hurried after her.

The police officers took their names, addresses, and phone numbers.

"Good thing you guys went hunting for the girl," one of the officers said. "It looks like she needed help fast."

"You think she'll be okay, don't you, Julio?" Mona asked as they made their way back to the street.

Julio shrugged. "I hope so. She looked like my uncle did when he had a heart attack."

Abel's face was disfigured with sorrow. It was not that he loved Bianca Marquez. But when he was so sad from losing the girl he *did* love, Claudia Villa, Bianca came along to give him solace.

"Why didn't her mother see what was happening?" Abel said to no one in particular, his eyes clouded with anger. He opened and closed his hands, making helpless fists. "She was wasting away, and her mother didn't even notice."

"Does she have a dad?" Mona asked. Mona did not think her parents were perfect by any means, but if she had gotten to look like Bianca, they would have both taken her to a doctor or therapist.

"Parents divorced," Abel said. "There's a stepdad there, some little creep who pays no attention to her. The bio dad, who knows where he's at." Abel turned to the others. "You guys, thanks for, you know, being there." He looked directly at Julio. "Thanks to you especially, dude. You know the park better than anybody, and you knew to check by the overlook. The rest of us might've skipped that."

Julio smiled. "That was home to me and Pop many a night, man. Just because it was so secluded," he said.

Mona climbed in the old truck with Julio, and he drove her to her condo on Cardinal Street. She wished she could ask him inside to meet her parents, but she didn't dare. They sat in the cab for a few minutes, though, and finally Mona reached over and grasped Julio's hand and gave it a squeeze. "Your buddies are really high on you, Julio. I can see why," she said.

Julio turned and gave Mona a kiss on the cheek. It was the sweetest thing that

Mona could remember ever happening to her, and she tingled all over. All the way to her door, and even inside, she continued to tingle.

When Mona walked inside and closed the door, her mother called in a nervous voice, "Mona? Is that you?"

"Yeah, Mom, I'm home," Mona said.

Mrs. Corsella came into the front room, her eyes wide, "What's going on? I was so worried about you. You sounded so mysterious on the phone, and then I heard a lot of sirens up on Washington Street and …" she said.

"Mom, something happened to one of the seniors, and we all sorta hung around until the paramedics came," Mona said, changing the story to make it more acceptable to her mother. Her mother would never have approved of Mona being part of a search party, crawling around the ravine looking for a missing girl. She wouldn't understand what had happened at all.

"*What*?" Mrs. Corsella asked, looking

alarmed. "Who was the senior? Is it someone we know?"

"I don't think you know her, Mom. Her name is Bianca Marquez. Her family lives right down the street here, but I've never even talked to her before. She's in some of my classes. Anyway, she's got this thing about wanting to be super skinny like the girls you see modeling clothes and stuff. Her boyfriend thought she had anorexia, and he called her mother, but she wouldn't do anything. Anyway, the kid sorta collapsed, and we wanted to make sure she was okay."

"Is she going to be all right?" Mrs. Corsella asked.

"We don't know. They took her to the hospital," Mona said.

"Oh my goodness, how terrible," Mrs. Corsella said, and then her expression changed. "Did anything else interesting happen today, Mona?"

In all the excitement over Bianca, Mona had forgotten Louis Oriana and the plot her mother had hatched for him to ask her out. Mona laughed a little and decided to go along with the farce. "Oh yeah, Mom, some really weird guy asked me if I wanted to go out for pizza after school. I think his name was Louis or something. Anyway, I've seen him around school with some other nasty creeps, and they make fun of girls who aren't cute. I hate guys who do that. I mean, I wouldn't walk to the corner of the street with a little weirdo like that. I told him to get lost."

Mrs. Corsella looked horrified. "But Mona … that was … so rude. I'm sure he's not as bad as you say he is," she stammered.

"Oh, he is, Mom. His best friends are Clay Aguirre and Rod Garcia, and they're the biggest jerks in the senior class. Who needs somebody like that?" Mona said.

Mrs. Corsella just stood there, her hands intertwining frantically.

CHAPTER FIVE

Later in the day, after Xavier Corsella got home, Mom said, "Mona, I was waiting for you to come home, and I happened to see you dropped off from a beat-up, old green truck. I expected you to be taking the bus, and this old rust bucket rolled to the curb, then you got out. I don't recall ever seeing it before."

"Oh yeah, we were all so worried about Bianca that we missed our usual rides. I missed the bus, and this guy offered me a ride home. I just jumped in. Julio is in my classes at Chavez. He's a senior too," Mona said.

"Julio?" Mrs. Corsella repeated the

name. "Have you mentioned him before? I don't remember you talking about a Julio."

"Oh, he's the star of the Cesar Chavez track team. He's a super athlete, Mom. He won the three-mile championship last weekend in Balboa Park. Coach Muñoz is really excited about him leading the Cougars to a regional championship," Mona said.

Mona's father had been working on the computer, but now he looked up. "I read about that boy in the sports section of the paper," he said. Mona didn't know many people anymore who got their news from the morning paper, but Dad loved his newspaper. "Was a real nice article about him. I took notice because you don't often read about kids from Chavez High. That would be Julio Avila, right?"

"Yeah," Mona said.

Mom's expression changed from interest to distaste. "Oh, Mimi and I have talked about that family. Isn't the boy's father a panhandler?" Mom's voice was sharp and critical.

Mona felt sick. She was sorry she'd ever mentioned Julio's name at all, but sooner or later, she'd have to tell her parents about her friend. "Mom, Mr. Avila doesn't do that anymore. He's disabled from the merchant marine, and they're very poor. But Julio has a good job at the supermarket, and they're doing better. Mr. Avila is a nice man, and his son loves him very much," Mona said.

Mom continued scowling, "Well, that's all well and good, and I suppose you had no choice in accepting a ride from him this once, but I'd rather you stayed away from him. They're not our kind of people. Mimi told me that Julio is a very tough boy, and he hangs out with the wrong crowd."

"Mom," Mona whined, "Julio's best friends with Ernesto Sandoval, our senior class president, and Abel Ruiz!"

"Well," Mrs. Corsella said, "if I were Ernesto's and Abel's parents, I'd encourage them to choose better friends than that Avila boy. The downfall of many good kids in the *barrio* is bad companionship. Ernie and Abel are fine young men, but they are risking their reputation to be with a boy like that."

"You know what, Mom?" Mona said bitterly. "When you talk about bad companions, I think of you hanging with Mrs. Oriana and the other women who play bunco in your group. Her son hangs with the most evil creeps at school, and when you guys are playing bunco, all I ever hear from you is gossip. 'Oh, did you hear about Emily's husband? Cheating again,' or 'Did you see that new car the Pinedas have? I think Mr. Pineda plays fast and loose with investment money.' "

"Young lady," Mrs. Corsella said, "do not talk to me in that tone of voice." She turned to Mona's father. "Xavier, haven't you anything to say or do you approve of your daughter talking to me in that nasty, sassy voice?"

Mr. Corsella looked up from the computer and said wearily, "Mona, don't argue with your mother. We have enough trouble with the shaky real estate market. We don't need any more stress in this family. There are plenty of nice young men at Chavez High, so you don't need to upset your mother by hanging with the Avila boy."

Mona muttered, "I'm sorry, Mom," and fled to her room. She was not really sorry. That was the most insincere voice she had ever used in her life. And she had no intention of ending her friendship with Julio Avila. It probably wouldn't amount to anything anyway, but as long as Julio wanted to be friends with Mona, she was going to be friends with him.

"I'm almost eighteen years old," Mona thought to herself. "And I've never had a real boyfriend in my whole life. Mom's not going to ruin this for me."

At school the next day, Ernesto and Naomi approached Mona. "We went down to the hospital last night to see Bianca. Abel was there already," Ernesto said.

"How is she doing?" Mona asked.

"Bianca is anorexic all right," Naomi said. "She weighs only eighty-eight pounds! The doctors are gonna keep her in the hospital for a few days, then she'll be treated in an outpatient program. She has to see a psychologist. The doctor said it was a good thing she got into treatment now before her heart and kidneys were affected."

"Wow," Mona said.

"Abel is really ticked off at Bianca's mom," Ernesto said. "But I was so proud of the guy. Mrs. Marquez came over and just apologized all over the place, and she wants all our addresses so she can do thank-you notes and stuff. In spite of how he feels, Abel held his anger back and was almost cordial. Almost, but not quite." Ernesto grinned. "Parents can be pretty clueless sometimes," he added.

"You can say that again," Mona said. She turned and headed for Mr. Davila's class. On the way, she ran into Louis Oriana. He smirked when he looked at her.

"Hey, I'm sorry if I offended you yesterday asking you to go for pizza," he said in a sarcastic voice.

"You didn't offend me," Mona said. She could tell that Louis wasn't really apologizing. He had an ulterior motive.

"I was just trying to do you a favor, you know. Kind of like a good deed," he said.

"I don't need any favors," Mona snapped.

"Oh yeah?" Louis continued. "I don't exactly see the dudes fighting each other to take you out, girl."

Mona Corsella was shy, but when rage took over, she turned into a whole different person. "You know what, Louis Oriana? If I never had a date in my entire life and you were the only guy on the planet, I wouldn't touch you with a ten-foot pole. You totally creep me out."

Anger turned the boy's face red. He was mad that he had done what his mother asked, and this was the thanks he got.

"You dog," Louis hissed at Mona. "No guys want to take dogs out, didn't you know that? Who do you think you are? Why don't you go look in the mirror?"

Julio Avila came walking along just as Louis had finished talking. Julio could tell something ugly was going on, but he hadn't heard anything. "What's going down?" he asked.

"Nothing," Mona said. "I'm going to history class."

Julio turned to Louis Oriana. "You were hassling her, weren't you, dude?" Julio was six foot plus and a solid one hundred eighty pounds. Louis Oriana was about five ten, and if he weighed one forty, it was a stretch.

"No, I wasn't doing anything," Louis said. He was visibly nervous. Julio was not only big and ripped, but he had the reputation of being hot-tempered and even dangerous if provoked.

"Listen up, man," Julio said, his face getting close to Louis's. "You bother this chick and I'm gonna take it out of your hide, understand? I've seen you and Aguirre and

Garcia perched on the fence like vultures making ugly comments about girls. You make me sick, man, and when I get sick, I'm likely to do bad things, okay?"

"Hey, don't sweat it," Louis said. "I'm out of here. I don't want any trouble."

Mona was shocked. Julio was fighting mad because he thought some dude had harassed Mona. She and Julio hardly knew each other, and here he was defending her!

"Julio," Mona said, "I don't want you to get into a hassle over me. I mean, I can handle jerks like him."

Julio had looked like a madman only a moment ago, his dark eyes smoking, his nostrils flaring, but now he flashed a grin that transformed his face. He reached out with his left hand and gently took Mona's chin between his thumb and index finger. "Babe, get used to it," he said. "Nobody trashes a chick I like."

Mona could hardly concentrate on history during Mr. Davila's class. She thought about Julio for the rest of the day, and as she rode the bus home, she was still thinking about him.

When Mona walked into the condo, she was surprised to see her younger brother, Peter, sprawled on one of the overstuffed chairs. He jumped up and grabbed Mona, lifting her off her feet. "Hey, *hermana*, you look great," he said. "You're even prettier than I remember. *Muy hermosa!*"

"Oh, it's so good to see you, Peter," Mona cried, kissing him. "I missed you so much!"

"I got a week's leave. Boot camp is over and somehow I survived. It looks like I'm really gonna be one of the few and the proud!"

Dad wasn't home yet, but Mom came into the room and said, "Peter, I didn't think you'd be here until tomorrow. My bunco group is coming over, and you know how the girls drive you crazy."

Peter laughed. "Oh man. The bunco biddies."

"They are not biddies," Mom scolded

with a smile on her face. "Most of them are not even fifty!"

Peter turned to Mona. "How about if you and me cut out for a movie and pizza or something?"

"Oh, wow, Peter, that'd be so cool," Mona said.

"Can I use one of the family limos, Mom?" Peter asked.

"Of course. You can use my Honda, dear," Mom said.

As Peter and Mona drove out in the Honda, Mona said, "Oh, look, one of the biddies is arriving already. That's Mimi Oriana, remember her?"

"Oh yeah," Peter said, "one of the worst gossips in the American West."

"Yeah," Mona said. "It isn't about bunco at all. It's about gossip. They get really upset if there isn't a couple of them missing, because it's more fun if they can gossip about whoever isn't there. Oh, Peter, my life is getting really strange, and I'm just bursting with stuff I wanna talk about."

"Let it rip, *hermana*," Peter said. "The minute I saw you today, I saw something different about you. Your eyes sparkle in a special way. I'm guessing now, but there's a dude, right?"

"Well, sorta," Mona said. "You know I never had a real boyfriend before 'cause I'm not—"

"No way I'm buying that, *hermana*," Peter cut in. "You're a cute girl, Mona. You don't look like all the *other* hot chicks because you got a unique look, but it's just as appealing as any other girl. It's like some actresses. They don't look like the rest, but they're pretty anyway."

"Peter, I love you for saying that even though it isn't true," Mona said. "But the thing is, there *is* a boy who's interested in me now, and I'm getting to like him so much. I think about him all the time. He's cute and athletic, and he's really nice," Mona said.

"But …" Peter said. "There's a 'but' isn't there? There is always a 'but.'" Peter was grinning at his little sister. "Let's hear it."

"Well, Mom is the problem. She doesn't even know how I feel about this boy, but she saw him driving me home once, and when she found out who he was, she got all bent out of shape," Mona groaned.

"So, what's she got against the guy?" Peter asked.

"Well, Mom has this horrible bigoted attitude against people who don't have the same kind of life we do. This boy comes from a really poor background, and he's had a rough life. He isn't bad or anything, but his father, you know, he's sorta disabled, and sometimes he'll ask for money. I mean, he's not a bum or anything," Mona wailed. "But the boy is so kind and wonderful and …"

"Okay, Mona," Peter said. "Let's cut to the chase. Who is this dude, and what has Mom *really* got against him?"

"Well, he and his father live in a little trailer in that run-down part of Oriole, and before that they were kinda homeless for a while. The dad doesn't work, but my friend works at the supermarket, and he kinda supports his father. Mom, she thinks we're high class or something, and she looks down on people who are like living on the edge and stuff," Mona said.

"Well, I'm getting the picture, Mona, but I still don't know who the dude is. Does he go to Cesar Chavez High School? Maybe I know him. If he's a senior now, then he probably was a freshman when I was a senior," Peter said.

"You probably wouldn't know him, Peter," Mona said. "He doesn't have a lot of friends. His name is Julio Avila." Mona looked for a sign of recognition in her brother's face.

"Yeah, *yeah*," Peter said. "I remember the kid. He was a brash handsome dude, tall for his age. He was tall for a freshman, and he could run like the wind. I remember tangling with him one time, and it was like getting in a fight with a buzz saw. That dude wouldn't take anything off of anybody."

"Oh no," Mona wailed. "Don't tell me you don't like him either. I thought maybe you'd be on my side, Peter!"

"Mona, chill! I didn't say I didn't like him. I actually grew to respect Julio a lot. I remember his mom was long gone, and he lived with his father who was this hobo type. The dad came to school one afternoon dressed in his raggedy clothes and not smelling too good, and some dudes were hassling him and calling him bad names. Along comes this little fourteen-year-old, and he comes on like a tornado, standing up for his father." Peter stopped to look at his sister.

"Here was this older dude, wearing jeans with holes in the knees, a red sweater and a purple coat, looking like a cross between a clown and street person, and most fourteen-year-olds would've been so ashamed of a father like that. They wouldn't have admitted this awful-looking guy even *was* their dad. Not Julio. He stood up for his father and beat off the dudes who were giving the guy a hard time," Peter said.

"I'm telling you, Mona, even the seniors were afraid of crossing Julio. I had a lot of respect for him after that. I imagined having a father like that myself, coming around the school and embarrassing me. Man, I would've taken off in the other direction. So, Mona, I like the guy," Peter said. "I haven't seen him in years, but if he's half the dude he was when he was fourteen, then he's a class act."

"Oh, Peter, he's still like that. He loves his father so much. I went to the race in Balboa Park on Sunday, and Julio won the three-miler, and there was his dad, tears in his eyes, just clapping like crazy. Julio walked right up to him in front of everybody and gave him a big hug," Mona said.

"Good for him," Peter said.

"You know, Peter, Mom has always been embarrassed that I don't have a big, busy social life like she had at my age. She doesn't know about me and Julio, so she got creepy Mimi Oriana to have her son, Louis, ask me to go for pizza after school.

Mom thought she could get something going between me and Louis, but, honestly, I'd rather be dead! Anyway, Louis was peeved when I turned him down, and today he started calling me ugly names and stuff, and Julio came along, and, wow, Julio scared Louis silly. I couldn't believe that Julio is so into me that he'd defend me like that. I was blown away, Peter," Mona said.

"Well, Mona, if you like Julio, stand your ground. If Mom is giving you trouble, just be polite and nice, but stand up for yourself. It's your life, girl," Peter said.

"Oh, Peter, I love you so much," Mona cried, kissing her brother's cheek. "And I'm proud of you and Jimmy too. You're my heroes."

Peter turned and smiled at his sister as he parked in the mall where the movie theater was.

Mona thought that today was one of the best days of her entire life.

When Peter and Mona got home, the last of the bunco women were leaving.

The moment the last one was gone, Mrs. Corsella turned to her son and said, "Peter, we have a problem with your sister. She insulted Mimi Oriana's son, and she's turning into a hard, disrespectful girl."

CHAPTER SIX

M om," Peter said, taking his mother in his arms and hugging her. "Don't worry your sweet head over such nonsense. Mimi Oriana is a nasty old gossip, and she has always been one. No doubt she exaggerated what Mona said to her son. Poor Mimi is not a happy woman, so she spreads tales of woe to make everyone as miserable as she is. Come on, *mi madre*, be happy. Your *hijo* is home, your beautiful daughter has roses in her cheeks, and soon the houses will be selling like fish tacos on a Friday afternoon, and you will be rich again!"

In spite of herself, Martha Corsella started to laugh too. She couldn't resist the charm of her youngest son. "Oh, Peter, you are so bad," she giggled.

"Mrs. Oriana reminds me of the crows, Mom. You see them flying across the sky, then they all settle on the trees and start babbling and scolding. Some poor crows were already sitting on the branches nice and peaceful like, and now they're all fighting because some crows and some people just like to spread trouble. So, *mi madre*, what delicious snack do you have for your hungry Marine? We ate popcorn at the movies, but we're still hungry," Peter said.

"*Mi hijo*," Martha Corsella said, "I served the girls nice barbecued chicken, and I was about to put the leftovers back in the fridge but—"

"Bring it on, Mom," Peter said.

Xavier Corsella then came in the house in unusually high spirits. He worked later tonight than he had in months. "I closed the deal, Martha," he exulted. "I sold the house on Wren Street! Going to be my first commission in three months!"

"That's wonderful," Mrs. Corsella cried. "It's the house next door to the Sandovals, isn't it?"

"Yes, yes, and the credit goes to Luis Sandoval. There's a new teacher at Chavez, and Luis talked her into looking at the house next door to his, which I happen to have the listing on. Connie Medina, that's the teacher. I think she fell in love with the house because she and her husband will have such great neighbors! The Medinas have two little girls, preteen, and they'll be great friends of the Sandoval girls."

Mona's dad turned to her. "And there's good news for you too, sweetheart. The Medinas have an older son who's a senior at Chavez, a fine boy. I showed him your picture, and he seemed quite interested. He wants to meet you, Mona. His name is Barney."

Mona wanted to say something spiteful, but she held her tongue. She exchanged a look with Peter and tried to enjoy the barbecued chicken.

"What am I?" Mona thought to herself bitterly. "Some white elephant everybody is trying to pass off?" Mona did not want to meet Barney Medina or anybody else. She was growing to like Julio Avila more each minute, and all she wanted was for her mother and father to leave her alone to live her life.

The next day, Martha Corsella said to Mona, "This weekend, the Sandovals are having a little get-together at their house to introduce the Medinas to their friends. It'll be on Sunday afternoon. Maria asked us to come, Mona. You'll get to meet Barney Medina then. He's really anxious to meet you."

"I don't want to meet anybody, Mom," Mona said, trying to keep the anger from her voice.

"Why not, dear?" Mom said. "The only social life you have now is some silly infatuation with that street person's son, and we both know that's going nowhere."

"I gotta get to school," Mona snapped. "The bus will be here in a coupla minutes."

Mona grabbed her backpack and ran down the street to the corner where the bus picked up the kids for Chavez.

When Mona got to school, she looked around for Carmen Ibarra. Carmen was dating a guy about twenty who managed an electronics store. He was really tough, a little like Julio. He even had a rattlesnake tattooed on his hand. Carmen told a lot of stories about how unhappy her parents were when she started dating this guy— Paul Morales. But little by little, they came around and accepted Paul. Now Mona wanted to ask Carmen how she got Paul into the good graces of her parents.

Carmen was walking with Naomi Martinez when Mona caught up to them. "Oh, Carmen, you gotta help me," she said.

"Okay, Mona, what's up?" Carmen asked.

"Carmen, I really, *really* like Julio Avila, but my mom hates him. She doesn't even know him, but she hates his father for the way he is, and she thinks Julio is trash. Mom is so stuck up. She thinks we're high class or something, and Julio's father sometimes asks for handouts and stuff, and Mom really looks down on that. And Mom thinks Julio is tough and crude. You said your parents didn't like your boyfriend at first, and I gotta know what you did to bring them around," Mona said.

"Oh," Carmen said, "Paul is much worse than Julio. My father really flipped when he saw him, especially when he saw the snake tattoo on his hand. I thought Dad was going to pass out. And my older sister was terrified of Paul. She thought he was a gangbanger. But what I did was, I invited Paul over for dinner at my house, and my parents like freaked, but once they met him, it got a little better. But it was still a struggle for a long time." Carmen paused to breathe.

"Now it's really good. Paul is like part of the family. His brother, David, works in my father's office. So, Mona, you gotta get them together, Julio and your parents. It's easy to hate somebody you don't even know, but when they're sitting across the dinner table from you, then it's harder to hate them."

"Ohhh," Mona groaned. "Mom would never let me bring Julio to the house, much less serve him dinner. My father might go along with that, but he won't either 'cause he doesn't want to rile Mom. On Sunday, Mom is going to introduce me to some jerk named Barney Medina. She's bound and determined that I forget Julio and go with somebody I don't know."

"Here comes Ernie," Carmen said. "He's the one to solve your problem, Mona."

"Yeah," Naomi said. "Ernie can do anything. My father and my brothers were such bitter enemies. They hadn't talked in years, and Ernie helped me bring the family together again."

When Ernesto arrived, Carmen related Mona's problem, talking a mile a minute as she usually did.

"Oh man," Ernesto said, a thoughtful look on his face. Then he said, "I think I have a plan."

"See? *See*?" Naomi cried. "Didn't I tell you he could do anything? Ernie thinks he can save the world, one person at a time, and so far he's having pretty good luck."

Ernesto laughed. "Not quite," he said. "But this get-together where you're supposed to meet Barney Medina is gonna be at *my* house, Mona. We're supposed to introduce the Medinas to all the neighbors and our friends. Abel Ruiz is coming, and the Ibarras, and well, Julio and his dad are my friends, so I'll just invite them too."

"Oh my gosh," Mona gasped, "would you do that, Ernie?"

"Sure," Ernesto said. "Julio is one of my favorite homies. He's often hanging at our house. So the Medinas can meet him. Your mom and dad will be there too, Mona, and we'll all be munching on Mom's scrumptious empanadas and the iced tea will be flowing. Good feelings all around."

"Oh, my mom will be so furious," Mona said. "But she and Dad have good manners. They'll be polite even if they have to talk through gritted teeth. And I gotta believe they'll soften to Julio when they see him and his dad. Oh, Ernie, thank you so much."

"*Por nada*," Ernesto said. "Julio is a nice guy, and his father is quiet and sweet. Who wouldn't like them?"

"Oh, you guys, I'm so happy," Mona said. "I really think this is gonna work!"

As Sunday loomed, Mona was having serious doubts about Ernesto's plan. She thought it might all just blow up in her face. It was an informal little party for the new neighbors, and Martha Corsella did not dream Julio Avila would be there, let alone his hobo father. But the Avilas *were* neighbors, in a sense, though the little trailer park at the end of Oriole was quite a distance away.

Because Xavier knew the Medinas best, having shown them the house they were buying, he, Martha, and Mona arrived first at the Sandoval house. Their house was small but tastefully decorated and not crowded with furniture. There was plenty of space for all the people who would come. Among the sofas, easy chairs, and folding chairs were coffee tables for the food.

Mona spotted the Medinas coming down the walk. Connie Medina was a well-built lady, and her husband was tall and skinny. Their younger girls were not with them, but a chubby boy about eighteen followed them. Mona figured that was Barney. She disliked him immediately, though she knew that was unfair because she didn't even know him. What's more, she didn't *want* to know him. She didn't want to become his or anybody else's girlfriend, not since she met Julio.

Linda, Felix, and Naomi arrived next, followed by Emilio and Conchita Ibarra and Carmen. Liza and Sal Ruiz came with Penelope and Abel.

Maria and Luis Sandoval were engaged

in happy chatter with all their guests when Mona noticed that Ernesto was missing. Then the Volvo pulled up, discharging not only Ernesto, but also Julio Avila and his father. Mona's heart stopped, or seemed to anyway.

Carmen and Naomi exchanged a nervous look.

Ernesto and the Avilas came in the door quickly. Mona was pleased to see that Mr. Avila was dressed more nicely than usual. He wore a nice, clean polo shirt and pressed slacks. He almost looked normal.

"Hi, everybody," Ernesto said in his usual gregarious voice. "This is Mr. Avila and his son, Julio. Julio is an ace runner on the Cougar track team. We're counting on him to bring the championship to Chavez this year."

"Oh, my," Connie Medina said, glancing at her son, Barney. "Now that's what you need to do. Get on a track team."

Mona didn't want to look at her parents but she was forced to by the same instinct that compels a rabbit to stare into the face of a coyote waiting to devour it. Mom looked shocked and horrified. Dad looked dumbfounded. The get-together was going downhill fast when Felix Martinez loudly engaged the Medinas in conversation. "So, Connie, you gonna teach at Chavez like Luis here, huh? And, Mike, what do you do? You in the teaching racket too?"

"I'm a salesman," Mike Medina said. "School supplies."

"Well," Felix Martinez aid, "you're gonna have nice neighbors here. They don't come any better than the Sandovals. All in all, it ain't a bad *barrio*. A few taggers, gangbangers, but we ain't had a shooting in a while. Your kid there, Bunny, is that his name?"

"Barney," the young man said. "My name is Barney." He was looking around the room for the girl he had seen in the picture from the real estate man's wallet. His gaze fixed on Mona, and he achieved a dreamy smile. Mona looked away.

Abel and Penelope directed everyone to the food and drink.

Mike Medina's gaze settled on Julio and his father. "I saw an article about you in the sports section of the paper," he said. "You won that race in Balboa Park. You ran the three-mile course in record time too. Good for you. It's time Latino boys start making their mark in track," he said, turning then to Julio's father, who looked about as comfortable as a mouse in a trap. "So, you're retired, Mr. Avila?"

Mr. Avila's watery eyes widened in his prematurely lined face. "I'm on disability. Was in the merchant marine for a long time and hurt my back."

"Oh, sorry to hear that," Mr. Medina said.

Felix Martinez chimed in eagerly. "You talk about back trouble, try being a fork-lift operator and working on a construction site. Sal Ruiz, over there, he's in the land-scaping business, and he knows what bad backs are too, eh, Sal?"

Sal Ruiz was just getting over a terrible auto accident, and he nodded. "You can say that again, Felix."

"You'll love it around here," Luis Sandoval said to the Medinas. "You couldn't find a friendlier bunch of folks anywhere. Any problem comes up, and we're all family."

"That's the truth," Abel Ruiz said. "When my dad got hurt and was in the hospital, everybody came to help."

"We used to live here years ago," Luis Sandoval said. "Then we moved to Los Angeles. We're only back about a year and a half, and it's like we've been here all our lives. Everybody just wrapped their arms around us, the Martinezes, the Ibarras, the Ruizes."

Ernesto joined the conversation, "Yeah, when I started at Chavez High, I felt like a real outsider, but then Abel Ruiz comes along to befriend me, and Julio Avila, Carmen, a bunch of kids I didn't even know." Ernesto turned to Barney, "You'll find out that Chavez High is a terrific school, Barney. In fact, here's my invitation right now. You gotta come eat lunch with our gang, with me and Naomi, Carmen, Julio, Abel."

Mona stole nervous glances at her parents. They looked grim, especially Mom. If she had swallowed a lemon, she couldn't look worse. She cast dirty looks at Julio and his father, as if they were rats that had somehow gotten into her clean kitchen.

Emilio Zapata Ibarra said, "Ernie is right. We are all brothers and sisters here." As he spoke, his large mustache twitched.

"Emilio is our councilman," Maria Sandoval said. "And he's done so many wonderful things. We're all proud of him."

"A councilman," Connie Medina said, impressed. "Perhaps you could speak to my classes at school sometime."

"My pleasure, dear lady," Mr. Ibarra said.

Naomi turned to Julio and said, "Coach

Muñoz is so happy with how the track team is doing. This might be his last year at Chavez, and he said he wants to go out on top, and because of you, Julio, and the other guys, he just might."

Julio, who had been rigidly silent until now, smiled at Naomi and said, "He's a great coach. He deserves to go out a winner."

Mona sneaked another look at her mother. "Maybe," Mona thought, "she was softening." The atmosphere here was so nice and warm. Ernesto was talking to Barney about sports. Even the Medinas were including Julio and his father in their conversation.

But, no, Martha Corsella looked even angrier. She met Mona's gaze, and her eyes flashed hot. Mona could tell what her mother was thinking. This was a setup. Mona conspired behind her back to make this happen. She got Ernesto to bring in that nasty punk and his wretched father just to try to make them look respectable.

Mona's heart sank. It wasn't working out like Carmen said happened when she brought her boyfriend home to the Ibarra house. The Ibarras' hearts were more open.

As the little party was coming to an end, Barney Medina made his move. Mona did not hate him like she hated Louis Oriana. Louis was a nasty person, but poor Barney had been sand-bagged. His parents wanted to do a favor for the nice real estate agents who sold them the house by having their son take out the realtors' daughter. Barney was more than willing to play his part. And, if truth be told, he did think Mona Lisa Corsella was kind of cute. Barney had a weight problem and wasn't exactly the hottest teenager he knew.

"Mona," Barney said, "do you like jazz?"

"Not much," Mona said. "I like rap music and rock."

"Your father said so many nice things about you, Mona," Barney said. "You seem so nice. I thought maybe you'd enjoy

103

going out with me sometime to a concert. We could go to a rap or rock concert if you like."

"Thanks so much, Barney," Mona said, smiling at him. "You seem like a really cool guy, and I'd probably take you up on your offer but, see, I sorta got a boyfriend."

Barney Medina looked surprised. "Oh. Your father—"

"Yeah," Mona said. "I know. Mom and Dad are always trying to set me up with people. Mom doesn't think I have enough friends. But, look, Barney, if I were looking to go out with a new guy, you'd be at the top of my list."

Barney smiled warmly and walked away.

Naomi, Carmen, and Ernesto had tipped off their parents about how much it meant to Mona Corsella to have Julio and his father accepted, so they were all doing their best. It touched Mona so much to see Felix Martinez go over to Mr. Avila to talk about serving on the sea. Mr. Martinez was briefly in the U.S. Navy. Felix clapped the man on the back and told him maybe they could go fishing together sometime.

Emilio Ibarra chatted with Julio and his father, and so did Luis Sandoval. Sal Ruiz and Mr. Avila traded horror stories about failed remedies for their aching backs.

When all the thank-yous were said, and everybody was wending their way to their cars, Martha Corsella turned to her daughter and said, "You had it all planned, didn't you, Mona? I am just so shocked and disappointed that you would pull something like this, that you'd conspire with your friends to do this, knowing how your father and I feel. And I'm not very impressed with Ernesto Sandoval either, going along with it, bringing those disreputable Avilas into a nice gathering." Martha glared at her daughter.

"Mimi Oriana has told me Julio hangs out with very unsavory characters, and I believe it. Well, young lady, it didn't work. You are not to have anything to do with

Julio Avila, *ever*. If you defy us, then you will lose your cell phone, your computer, everything. You can sleep on a mattress on the floor in a bare room! And that, Missy, is a promise!"

CHAPTER SEVEN

Mona Lisa Corsella called Ernesto Sandoval from the phone in her bedroom at home. Fortunately, both her parents were out with clients. "Ernie, I hate my mom," Mona cried. "She's so mean. She said I can't ever be with Julio. She's threatening to take away my laptop and my phone and to make me sleep on the floor!"

"Oh, wow, that's terrible," Ernesto said. "Julio and his dad were so nice at the party. Everybody liked them. What got her so ticked off?"

"Oh, Ernie, it's that old hag Mimi Oriana. She's always filling Mom's mind with disgusting gossip. She told Mom that Julio is a gangbanger and that his father is almost a criminal. My brother Peter was home on leave, but he had to go back to his unit, so there's nobody to help me! What'll I do, Ernie? I could just die!" Mona sobbed.

"Listen, Mona, don't give up," Ernesto said. "My mom and yours were friends when they were kids and teenagers. They go out shopping sometimes, and I'll ask Mom to talk to your mother and try to get through to her. Mom is pretty good with stuff like that."

"Oh, Ernie, I can't live like this. I feel like I'm in prison for something I didn't do. In five months, I'll be eighteen, and she's treating me like a bad ten-year-old!" Mona said. "If your mom could help, I'd be so grateful."

Maria Sandoval called Martha Corsella that evening and asked her if she'd like to go shopping down at the mall. Maria Sandoval said the shops were having excellent sales and that she had some good coupons she was willing to share. "I need new clothes for the baby, and Katalina and Juanita are growing out of their stuff so fast," she said.

"Well, I need some sweaters," Martha Corsella said. "And I need some decent-looking comfortable shoes too. I do so much walking while showing real estate that my feet hurt almost constantly. There has to be a pair of comfortable, good-looking shoes out there. So, sounds good, Maria."

In the early afternoon the next day, the two women shopped for about two hours. Then they went to the food court and ordered lunch.

"Martha," Maria Sandoval said, "there's something I wanted to talk to you about. I hope you won't take this in a bad way, but some of Ernesto's friends are saying that Mona seems so depressed at school and that the kids are worried about her."

Mrs. Corsella's face hardened. "I know. We're having a really bad time with her. She wants to date a boy we do not approve of. When I forbade it, she turned hostile and sullen. Maria, I am so proud of my two sons. They are in the Marines, you know, and I'm determined that Mona keeps out of trouble too," she said.

"Martha, the boy you are talking about is Julio Avila, right?" Mrs. Sandoval asked.

"Yes. He has a dreadful drug addict father, and everybody knows Julio is a wanna-be gangbanger. For years, the father and son lived in the ravine, Turkey Neck," Mrs. Corsella said, shaking herself as if even the thought of such people made her ill.

"Martha, we have known Julio for a long time. He is not a bad kid. His father drinks too much and smokes, but he doesn't use drugs. Julio works long hours after school at the supermarket, and he's won all kinds of awards as an excellent employee down there. The boy sacrifices to be a good runner for the Chavez Cougars. Coach Muñoz would not tolerate a boy on the team who wasn't on the up-and-up. I don't know many seventeen-year-olds who would work so hard and take care of a disabled parent like he does. My son, Ernie, is a close friend of Julio's."

Martha Corsella's expression hardened even more.

"Maria, we've been friends for a long time, and I don't want to offend you, but I must say this. I have a friend who thinks your son has some very bad companions. I know Ernesto is a fine boy and the senior class president, but Mimi said he rides around in a wildly colored van with really vile boys, and some of his friends have tattoos and wear gang colors. I'm sorry to be the bearer of bad news, Maria, but if I were you, I'd be very worried about Ernie. He is not the good boy you think he is. He might be on the road to very serious trouble."

Maria Sandoval took a long, deep breath, and then she said, "Martha, Martha, remember when we were in middle school and this catty little girl, Esmeralda, gossiped about everybody and turned us all against each other?"

"Yes, I remember but ..." Martha Corsella said.

"Martha, these stories that Mimi's telling are all half-truths. My husband always tries to help the kids at school, even those with problems. I know all about the boys Ernesto has befriended, boys like Cruz Lopez and Beto Ortiz, and because of Ernesto and his dad, those kids are now in trade school, and they're doing fine."

Maria continued, "Cruz Lopez comes from a desperately poor family. When his mother was dying last year, Cruz and his out-of-work dad with two little girls had *nothing* to eat. Ernie and Abel and some of their friends brought groceries over there almost every day. Yes, some of the boys shave their heads and wear hoodies, but they're not bad. They're just poor. Ernesto befriends kids who are at risk, as does my husband. Martha, thank God you and I have never been in the awful circumstances some of those boys have come from. But to pass judgment on a boy like Julio just because of the hard times he's had … I just don't think it's fair to Julio or to Mona," Maria Sandoval said.

"I'm sorry, Maria," Mrs. Corsella said, "but my first obligation is to protect my daughter against bad elements. Since Mona has been interested in Julio Avila, she has turned from a sweet, obedient child into a rude, sassy little witch. I won't stand for it."

"Well, Martha," Maria Sandoval said sadly, "you're Mona's mother. I'm just giving you my honest opinion. If you crack down on the girl so hard that she turns on you, then you will have lost her. If I were you, I'd ask Julio Avila to lunch, just you and him. I would talk to him and find out who he really is. I think if you listen in a fair way, you might even end up liking him."

"I wouldn't lower myself to the same level as him. He would end up ridiculing me. I know that kind. I see those young toughs on the street, sneering at decent people. It's a bad world out there, Maria, much worse than you think. I know you and your

113

husband are soft on some of these people. I think that's one of the problems in our society. I think we need to go back to the good old days when punks were thrashed. Julio Avila was laughing at us all the time we were at that party at your house. He felt he pulled something over on us. I could see it in his eyes," Martha Corsella said, finishing her beverage. "But he did not pull anything over on me. He will not touch my daughter. I swear to it."

When Maria Sandoval got home, she sank into the sofa and closed her eyes. She had left her shopping bags in the car. She'd get them later. She had a splitting headache. She didn't even see her son sitting there waiting for her to get home.

"No luck, huh, Mom?" he asked softly.

"How did you know?" Mrs. Sandoval asked. "That poor child, Mona. When I think of how the Ibarras gave Paul Morales a chance when they couldn't stand the sight of him. They did that for Carmen, their child. Emilio Ibarra was actually frightened of Paul, but he gave him a chance, for the sake of Carmen. Now the Ibarras love Paul like a son." Maria Sandoval shook her head. "I gave it my best shot, but it was like talking to a brick wall."

Mona realized her mother wasn't home from shopping yet, so she went into the den where her father was working on the computer, updating his listings. "Dad, you have to help me," she said. "Mom is ruining my life. She's threatened to make my life miserable if I'm friends with Julio, and it's not fair, Dad. He's a good person. Julio is a really good person. Please help me, Dad."

Xavier Corsella slid his chair back from the computer. Deep in his heart, he always thought his wife was too hard on the kids, but he never interfered. The boys now joked that boot camp wasn't as tough as doing Mom's chores. But with Mona, it was clearly worse. "Honey, I understand how you feel," he said. "But your mother is just dead set against that boy, and you'll just have to make the best of it."

Tears filled Mona's eyes. "Dad, please, please, help me. You can talk to her. You're my father. She has to listen to you. I just want to be friends with Julio at school. I have nowhere else to turn, Dad," she said.

"I don't want to get on your mother's wrong side, Mona. She's a very strong-minded woman," Mr. Corsella said.

"You're afraid of her," Mona almost shrieked. "You're so afraid of her you won't stand up to her even to help your own daughter! Don't I mean *anything* to you, Dad?"

The man looked deeply upset. Yes, he was afraid of Martha Corsella. He loved her, but she was always the boss. It was her way or the highway. She decided where they would live, where they would go on vacation, everything. "Mona, I'm sorry," he said, his voice barely above a whisper.

Mona turned and went to her room. There was just one hope left. Maybe Maria

Sandoval had been successful today in talking a little reason into her mother.

If that hadn't worked, then Mona knew she was against the wall. Little by little, desperation was taking over her mind and heart. It wasn't even that she cared so much for Julio Avila yet, though she thought it would come to that later. It was the principle of the thing.

All the other senior girls were living their lives, having fun, choosing their friends. As long as they didn't step over the line, use drugs or alcohol, hang with boys who were drug abusers or violent, their parents were reasonable. Mona did not know anybody on such a tight rein as she was.

Mona's mother came into the house at five thirty. She had a hard look on her face. She rapped on Mona's bedroom door. Even before Mona said she could come in, she entered.

"Mona, I was set up again today. Ernesto's mother, Maria Sandoval, pretended she wanted to go shopping with me, but what she really wanted to do was undermine my parenting. When we sat down for lunch, she unloaded all this garbage about what a fine boy Julio Avila was. Maria Sandoval is a very foolish woman who believes teenagers have the right to run wild and do anything they want to do. But I am not of that school of thought. I think you have been whining to Ernesto about what a mean person I am. Well, it didn't work, Missy. I have not changed my mind. Just because Maria Sandoval is okay with her son hanging out with the scum of the earth, I am not. You will have nothing to do with Julio Avila. At school, you will not have lunch with him or talk to him. Do you understand?"

Mona glared at her mother in silence.

"Don't look at me like that Mona Lisa Corsella," Mrs. Corsella said. "Don't give me that hateful look. Years from now, when you are married to a nice, decent man, you will get on your knees and thank me for protecting you from the likes of Julio Avila.

Barney Medina would love to take you out, and I cannot see why—"

"I wouldn't go out with Barney Medina or that horrible creep Louis Oriana if my life depended on it," Mona said. "I'd rather die than spend fives minutes with either of them."

"Don't you dare talk to me in that tone of voice, Mona," Mrs. Corsella said.

"I hate you," Mona said. Her voice was strangely calm.

"Well, if you don't apologize at once for that remark, young lady, you will lose your cell phone today. You think about it. In the morning, the phone will be gone. And that is only the beginning," Martha Corsella said.

Mrs. Corsella left her daughter's room and found her husband still at the computer. "Xavier," she said in a trembling voice, "Mona is turning into a monster. Can't you see that? Are you so clueless that you can't see what's happening to your own daughter?"

"Dear," Xavier Corsella said in a weak voice, "perhaps we are being a bit too hard on her ... if we—"

"Oh!" Mrs. Corsella cried. "I should have known better than to express my concerns with you. You want to be her friend, not her parent! Well, I'm willing to endure her hatred of me to save her from the likes of Julio Avila!"

That evening, both Corsellas had to go to a realtors meeting. They planned to be gone between seven thirty and nine thirty. When they left, Mona seemed to be doing homework.

The Corsellas returned home near ten o'clock. Martha Corsella believed that Mona had likely thought over her harsh remarks and was now ready to apologize. Mrs. Corsella was planning to extend her forgiveness if only Mona promised to avoid Julio Avila.

"Mona?" her mother called as she rapped on the door. There was no answer.

"Mona!" she repeated in a more strident tone. But there was still no answer. Mrs. Corsella turned the doorknob and went in the room.

And then she screamed.

Xavier Corsella came running, almost stumbling on a throw rug in the hallway. "What is it? What's wrong?" he cried.

"She's gone!" Mrs. Corsella screamed. "Look, the closet door is open. Her clothes are gone. She took her sweaters and jeans. Her purse. She ran away. Oh, Xavier, I never dreamed it would come to this! How did it happen? Only weeks ago, she was a nice little girl."

"She probably just went to stay with a girlfriend in the neighborhood," Mr. Corsella said.

Martha Corsella rushed to the phone. She called Mona's best friend, Teri Montina. "My daughter has run way," she cried. "Is she there with you?"

"No," Teri said. "Oh my gosh."

Mrs. Corsella called Naomi Martinez and

Carmen Ibarra. "I'm sorry, Mrs. Corsella," Naomi said, "but she's not here."

Felix Martinez took the phone from his daughter and said, "Hey, Martha, listen up. I ain't the sharpest knife in the drawer, but the way you been riding that little girl, I ain't surprised she took off. She's a good kid but you—"

Martha Corsella turned to her husband, her face twisted in fury. "She's with *him*! Why didn't I think of that right away? She's run away with Julio Avila! He must have come to the house when we were gone and taken her. I'm calling the police!"

"Martha, no," Mr. Corsella pleaded. "We don't know if anything of the sort happened. She may just be hiding out somewhere to cool down."

"I'm a mother," Mrs. Corsella cried. "I know something terrible has happened. That boy kidnapped her. I'm calling the police!" She dialed 911.

"Nine-one-one. What is your emergency?" the dispatcher asked.

"My daughter is missing. She's seventeen years old. My husband and I were away for two hours, and I think some criminal boy kidnapped her. Her bedroom is a mess. I think he forced her to go with him. His name is Julio Avila. He lives at the end of Oriole Street in a trailer park with his drug addict father. They're horrid people. They are capable of anything. I passed the wretched trailer once, but I don't know the number." Mrs. Corsella was frantic.

"Yes, my husband and I are on the way. We will meet the police there and rescue our daughter." Mrs. Corsella put down the phone. Her face was flushed, and she was trembling. "Come on, Xavier, the police are going there right away. We're going to meet them there. If only Mona is still there with him. Maybe he hasn't had time to take her somewhere else. Oh, the child must be frantic. Hurry, Xavier. *Will you hurry*?"

The Corsellas rushed out to their car and started down the street. "Oh, Xavier, I knew the boy was evil, but I never expected something this awful. She must have called him and said we were away, and then he probably made his move. He probably drove to our house and got her. Oh, Xavier, how can people like that live among decent people? This is so terrible." Martha Corsella cried, wringing her hands. "Xavier, can't you drive a little faster?"

"I'm already going over the speed limit," the man said.

The police cruiser had arrived moments before the Corsellas. When Martha and Xavier Corsella drove up to the sickly looking little green trailer where the Avilas lived, Julio Avila and his father were standing outside.

The police cruiser's lights glowed eerily in the darkness as two police officers began to question the man and his son.

"I think my daughter is inside the trailer," Martha Corsella cried. "She may even be tied up."

"Martha, Martha," Xavier Corsella said in an anguished voice. But Mrs. Corsella rushed ahead and interrupted the conversation the police officers were having with Julio and his father.

"My daughter is infatuated with this boy. My little girl has gone crazy over this wretched gangbanger boy, and when I forbade her to see him anymore, she disappeared. My husband and I were gone from the house, and he must have come and taken her," Mrs. Corsella cried.

Mr. Avila looked stunned. He had clearly had too many beers, and he had trouble standing erect. He leaned on the trailer. Julio was remarkably calm. "Mrs. Corsella, I have not seen your daughter since school today," he said.

"He's lying," the woman hissed. "He knows where my baby is." Xavier Corsella put his hand on his wife's arm but she shook him free. "Search the trailer!" she cried in a hysterical voice. "My baby is in there!"

CHAPTER EIGHT

Julio Avila turned and opened the small door to the tiny trailer. "Come on in, officers," he said. "You're welcome to look anywhere. It won't take you long." As Julio ushered the officers into the trailer, he was on his cell phone.

Inside the trailer was a bunk bed at one end, and a tiny dinette in the middle that folded down into another bed. There was a tiny stove and a small refrigerator, a sink and a very small bathroom. A few old cabinets overhung the sink. The officers spent about two minutes inside, and then they went back outside. As they emerged from the trailer, a Volvo came driving up. Ernesto Sandoval and his father, Luis Sandoval, got out. Luis

Sandoval walked over to Mr. Avila and shook his hand. Ernesto gave Julio a hug. Julio had given Ernesto a rundown on the phone regarding what was going on.

The older of the two police officers walked over to the Corsellas. "We've made a report, but it appears that it's a runaway situation. Your daughter has been missing less than two hours. Chances are she's holed up somewhere with friends. She'll probably be back before morning. That's what usually happens," the officer said.

Martha Corsella was in despair. The police were not taking this seriously. "Mona is a good girl," the woman wept. "She would not have just run away. She has lived a very sheltered life. Someone must have taken her away. She wouldn't have gone on her own. I know my daughter." The woman cast Julio a dark look. "He knows where she is!" she said.

"Ma'am," the officer said patiently, "there's no evidence implicating these people in your daughter's disappearance."

"Can't you take them down to the station and question them?" Mrs. Corsella asked. "At least question the boy. He's an unsavory character. Everybody knows that. That's why I forbade my daughter to go near him."

"Ma'am," the police officer said, "we've run a check on Mr. Avila and his son, and there are no warrants on either of them. What this looks like is a teenaged girl having a fight with her parents and running away. She's probably at a girlfriend's house."

"She has no real friends," Mrs. Corsella cried.

Paul Morales and Carmen Ibarra pulled up then in Paul's old Jaguar. They both got out and joined Ernesto and his father. Carmen took the initiative. "Mrs. Corsella, just in the past few weeks, Mona was coming out of her shell. She was so happy to be eating lunch with Ernie and me and Julio and Abel ... she finally belonged to a group of friends, and it meant so much to her," Carmen said.

"She was being drawn into a web of bad companions," Mrs. Corsella said. "It was like a spider's web, drawing her in." The woman looked distraught as the officers returned to their cruiser and started to leave. Martha Corsella was weeping. "Xavier, they're ignoring us. Our child is gone and they don't care."

Luis Sandoval drew closer to the Corsellas. He focused on Mr. Corsella because Martha was hysterical. "Xavier, what exactly happened? When did you last talk to Mona?"

The man looked guilty, almost grief stricken. "Mona came to me and begged me to help her. She was crying. I have never seen her so devastated. She begged me to, you know, intercede for her with her mother, but I … I refused. That was in the late afternoon, and then Martha and I had to go to a realtors meeting. When we returned home, around ten … she was … gone," he said.

Mr. Sandoval turned to Mrs. Corsella.

"When did you last talk to Mona, Martha?" he asked.

"Today, right before we left for the meeting. She was so awful. She told me she hated me. I threatened to take her cell phone away if she didn't apologize but … I never … saw her after that," Mrs. Corsella said.

Emboldened by the civil conversation the Sandovals were having with the Corsellas, Julio drew closer to Mona's parents. "Look," he said softly, "Mona and I were just like acquaintances. We met just a little while ago. She was so lonely. I like her. She watched me run in Balboa Park, and we ate barbeque at a little joint. We just talked and stuff like that. She never told me you guys hated me so much. I don't get it."

Mrs. Corsella glared at Julio Avila and said nothing.

"What about relatives," Ernesto said. "Grandparents or stuff. Sometimes kids run to them."

Xavier Corsella said, "My parents are

divorced. Mona was never close to them. Martha's mother lives in Florida. She never had a relationship with Mona."

"Anybody else?" Ernesto persisted. "Like an aunt or uncle she liked. I'm real close with my aunt Hortencia."

"I have a sister who lives in New Orleans," Martha Corsella finally said. "She's a weirdo. Never married. Mona has not seen her in seven or eight years. We went to Epcot when Mona was about ten, and we saw Aunt Corinne in New Orleans. She runs a mask shop. You know, for Mardi Gras. Mona seemed to like her, but she's really odd … I think Mona might have texted her a few times … I'm not sure."

"Well," Paul Morales said, speaking to the Corsellas for the first time tonight, "sometimes runaway kids go to the ravine. Turkey Neck. There's camps down there. Homeless dudes and runaways."

Mrs. Corsella looked horrified. "The ravine? That ugly, filthy place?" she gasped.

"Yeah," Paul said calmly. "Lotta kids

on the run end up there. There's sort of an encampment. We've found kids there and brought them home, right, Ernie? I'll get Cruz and Beto to help me look around."

Martha Corsella grabbed her husband's hand. "Oh, Xavier, our little girl in some filthy bum's roost?"

"Tell you what," Ernesto said. "Dad and Julio and Carmen and I, we'll go looking, and we'll call you right away if we find anything."

The Volvo carrying Ernesto and his father was followed by Paul's Jaguar with Julio and Carmen.

"Dude," Paul said, "that's one crazy lady. No wonder the poor kid cut out of there."

"Yeah," Julio said. "I was beginning to suspect Mona's mother didn't like me, so Ernesto sneaked me and Dad into a party at the Sandovals to meet her parents, but it didn't work out. I figured she was just a little leery of me, but it turns out she thinks I'm the scum of the earth, unfit to be near

132

her daughter. I'm thinking now I didn't do Mona any favors getting friendly with her, but I really like her."

"Mona needed friends," Carmen said.

"It was such a blast to see how excited she was when I took her to that little barbeque place. The kid is cute, she's a doll, but she's got this idea she's a dog," Julio said. "You know, some of my friends feel sorry for me that I don't have a mom. But I guess I'd rather have no mother around than a deal like Martha Corsella," Julio shook his head.

"I'm so lucky," Carmen said. "I've got great parents."

"Yeah," Paul agreed. "They really didn't like me at first, but they came around. Now I look at Emilio and Conchita as sorta my parents too. And then I look at Maria and Luis Sandoval as my parents too, so I end up with a bunch of nice moms and dads to make up for never having any real ones."

The five friends searched the ravine around Turkey Neck, but they found no sign of Mona Lisa Corsella. Ernesto called the Corsella home with the news. Martha Corsella had taken a tranquilizer and was resting, but Mr. Corsella accepted the news stoically.

Mona Lisa Corsella was never so lonely and frightened in her entire life. She huddled in her warmest coat in a seat midway back on the cross-country bus. With money she had saved from her pay at the yogurt shop added to gifts she got at Christmas from her grandmother in Florida and Aunt Corinne, Mona had enough to buy the ticket and have some left over for her needs.

Mona's parents knew that her grandmother always sent her twenty-five dollars for Christmas, but because they didn't like Aunt Corinne, the fifty-dollar gifts she sent were a secret between Mona and Corinne. Mona told her aunt to send the money to Teri Montina, and then Teri gave it to Mona. So, as she set out on her journey, Mona had three hundred dollars tucked in her bra.

About seven and a half years ago, the

Corsellas had gone to Epcot in Florida and also to see Mom's mother. On the way home, they detoured to New Orleans for a visit with Aunt Corinne. Martha Corsella did not especially want to see the woman she described as her "crazy sister," but her mother urged her to make the visit.

Mona had fallen in love with Aunt Corinne. Mona was bored by Epcot, and the visit to Grandmother was marked by a cold old lady complaining bitterly over her aches and pains, and how cruelly life had treated her. But Aunt Corinne was a pretty, vibrant lady with wild red hair and pink lipstick. She wore flamboyant costumes, and her mask shop was a spooky delight. It was a den of fascinating magic.

While her parents explored the sights of New Orleans, Mona stayed with her aunt and did not miss her parents for one minute. They rode horse-drawn carriages through the French Quarter and dined on fantastic Creole cuisine. Though Mona was only a little girl at the time, she had sworn to herself that she would go to live with Aunt Corinne one day.

And those many years ago, Mona had whispered in Aunt Corinne's ear that she wanted to come live with her.

"Fabulous," Aunt Corinne said, laughing, her bright pink lips spreading over her white teeth. "We'll have a ball, kid. Every day will be Mardi Gras. We'll rock Bourbon Street."

Mona didn't really think her aunt was serious—that it would be okay to come and live with her, but still, they did click. Ever since then, Aunt Corinne had sent little gifts, and they texted each other all the time. She seemed to really care about Mona.

And now Mona was in such desperate straits that she was going to Aunt Corinne, hoping she could hang with her until she turned eighteen. She had not called or texted Corinne to tell her she was coming. In fact, Mona did not even take her cell phone. She left it lying on her bedroom floor where she had thrown it in anger.

Mona Lisa just headed for Aunt Corinne in New Orleans, come what may, because she didn't know what else to do.

Mona wondered what her parents were doing right now. She felt guilty to be causing them worry, but she couldn't stand it anymore. The last straw came when her father wouldn't even stand up for her.

When the bus arrived in Phoenix, Arizona, Mona got off and walked around the bus station. She went out onto the street and stared at the tall buildings. When they had passed this way before almost eight years ago, there were fewer tall buildings.

"Hi there, beautiful," a young man said, coming alongside Mona. Startled, she turned. She didn't even see the guy until he was at her elbow. He was light-skinned, young, maybe twenty-five.

"My name is Tim Kent," the young man said, smiling. "I'm a photographer. I have a studio here in Phoenix. I'm on the lookout for fresh new faces for my advertising clients. I've got to say, you are stunning."

"Oh … thanks," Mona stammered. She did not believe him. She didn't think she was even pretty, much less stunning. Naomi Martinez was stunning. Mira Nuñez was stunning. "I'm just passing through. I'm going to New Orleans."

"Quite a ways to go yet," he said. "Well, listen, you don't have to get right on the next bus. You can take a detour and catch a later bus. My car is parked right on the street. I could drive you to my studio and take some publicity pictures and who knows where it might lead."

"I don't think so, thanks," Mona said. She had planned to get some breakfast here in the terminal. She was really hungry. Pancakes and sausage sounded good. "I'm going to get my breakfast now and …"

"Great," Tim Kent said. "I'll join you. In fact, it's on me. We can talk about the kind of work I do."

In the next few minutes, Mona was sitting at a table across from the young man and pouring maple syrup on her pancakes.

She bit a little brown sausage in two, and the grease ran down her chin. The young man reached over with a napkin and wiped Mona's chin. He smiled warmly at her and said, "You really have a unique beauty."

"Oh my gosh, no," Mona said.

"Listen, I've photographed a lot of girls, and I know what I'm talking about. I've done school yearbooks and portraits. I'm working up some photo portfolios now for some very big advertising programs. You've seen them on TV, bright young teen faces selling everything from cola to sunscreen. Right now, ethnic faces are hot. You're Hispanic, right?"

"Yes," Mona said.

"What's your name if you don't mind my asking?" the man said. "When I'm talking to somebody, I like to know her name," he asked.

"Mona ... Mona Corsella," Mona said.

"Well, nice to meet you, Mona. The thing is, Hispanic kids are really hot now. The Hispanic population is growing, you

139

know. The modeling agencies have lots of blonde, blue-eyed, white-bread girls, but a huge number of young girls don't identify with that look. They want to see themselves in the ads, and that's why I'm hunting for girls with exotic features like yours," he said, sipping his coffee.

"I, uh, thought that girls who wanted to be models took classes and stuff and submitted pictures," Mona said. "I never heard of somebody just seeing a nobody like me on the street and wanting to take their pictures," Mona said. She was suspicious. She just wanted to finish her breakfast and catch the bus for the next leg of her journey. It seemed preposterous to her that she had the looks for modeling. There had to be some mistake.

Tim Kent laughed. "Mona, you'd be surprised how many waste their money and take classes and spend a fortune on glossy portfolios, put their photos on Facebook, everything, but they just don't have the look that ad guys want. That's why I'm out here scooping up girls who have no idea how beautiful they are ... *girls like you.*"

Mona stared at the man. He wasn't handsome, but he was nice-looking. He had friendly clear blue eyes. Mona's misgivings faded a little, but she still wasn't sure she wanted anything to do with this.

"You have a haunting beauty, Mona," he said then.

Mona laughed. "I don't think so," she said.

"You know, Mona, here's the deal. If you're willing to come to my studio and just let me take a few photos, you can make an easy five hundred dollars," Tim Kent said.

"Five hundred dollars just for a few pictures?" Mona gasped.

"Yeah, and that's just the beginning," he said. "Why don't you take a shot, Mona? You have nothing to lose. There are buses going out every hour or so for New Orleans. Does it make a lot of difference if you get to New Orleans an hour late? Maybe this is your lucky day. We'll take

141

the pictures and put them out to my ad men, and they'll look at them right away and say yea or nay. Whatever happens, you get the five hundred dollars, which I figure you can use. I'm just guessing about this, Mona, but you're a runaway right?"

"No," Mona insisted in a frightened voice. "I'm going to visit family in New Orleans. My aunt lives there, and I haven't seen her in a long time. I'm going to spend some time with her 'cause she's all alone, and we've always been very close."

"Okay, Mona, fine. Just let me take my pictures, and you'll be on the bus in no time to visit your auntie," Tim Kent said.

Mona didn't know what to think. She thought it was probably some scam. After Tim Kent took the pictures, he would probably say that Mona had a lot of potential but that she needed a professional hairstyle and makeup and stuff before she could really make it, which would be expensive.

But maybe not. Maybe this was crazy enough to be the real thing. Maybe Mona

Lisa Corsella did have some strange kind of beauty that would sell cola or toothpaste. Maybe real kids out there would be more likely to buy stuff advertised by a fairly attractive girl who wasn't a stunning beauty.

"Maybe," Mona thought, "it was worth a shot." She could surely use five hundred dollars. When she appeared at Aunt Corinne's door, it would be nice to say, "Aunt Corinne, I don't expect you to support me. I've got some money to pay my way till I get a job."

And she could always catch the next bus.

CHAPTER NINE

How long did you say the pictures would take?" Mona asked.

He smiled warmly. "An hour at the most. Come on, my car is right at the door. I'll take you to the studio," he said.

"Yeah, well … okay, I guess," Mona said. "But I gotta get back here to catch the bus."

He led the way to his car and opened the door for Mona. He made sure she was buckled in before he started the car. Mona thought he was pretty nice.

"Boy," Mona said, "Phoenix is a really big city."

"Yeah. Every time they get a bad snow

year back east, we get a lot of new people."
He pulled into traffic.

"Do you do photography for magazines
or the Internet or …" Mona asked.

"Everything. You name it. You might
find yourself online before you know it,
Mona," he said.

"Wow, that's amazing," Mona said. "I
never thought of myself as pretty."

"I bet the dudes in college take a second
look at you," Tim Kent said.

"Oh, I'm not in college," Mona said.

"Oh. I just assumed you were skipping
out on the college drag. Lotta kids find
college a real hassle." They were already
on the freeway.

"I'm still in high school," Mona said.

The car was going down the off ramp.
Mona sensed the atmosphere in the car had
suddenly changed, grown colder. Tim Kent
wasn't smiling now. "High school," he
repeated, looking unhappy. He went down
a side street and pulled alongside a shoddy-
looking building. There were photographs

of girls outside, most wearing very little clothing. He turned and looked at Mona. "How old are you then?"

"I'm seventeen," Mona said, "but I'll be eighteen in a few months."

"Mona, you better get out of the car now and catch a local bus back to the terminal," the man said, no trace of a smile on his face. "You're underage."

"But … but, I can't even find the bus stop, or the one I need," Mona groaned. "I don't know Phoenix."

"Over there, across the street," the man said. He was out of the car, opening Mona's door.

"Please," Mona said, "can't you drive me back to the terminal?" She was trembling.

"Cross the street and a bus will be along in a few minutes. Come on, let's go," he said impatiently.

Mona got out of the car and crossed the street. She didn't know which bus to take, but when the first one stopped, she got on.

146

She asked the driver if this bus went to the terminal.

"You gotta transfer," the bus driver muttered. Mona sat down and waited for the stop. She was a nervous wreck. When the driver shouted the name of a street that sounded like her transfer spot, she jumped up and scrambled from the bus. The bus was pulling away when Mona stumbled on the curb and fell to her knees. Two middle-aged ladies came to her assistance.

"You okay, honey?" one of them asked.

"I think she's stoned," the other woman laughed. She smelled of alcohol and tobacco.

"I'm fine," Mona gasped. "I just bruised my knee a little, but it's okay."

The first lady patted Mona on the back and said, "Good luck, hon, these are mean streets."

Mona looked around, hoping to see the bus she needed. She touched the little bag pinned to her bra to reassure herself that her money was still there.

But the bag seemed so light!

Mona raced back to the spot where she fell. The contents of the little bag must have fallen into the street when she tripped. She found her driver's license and her school ID in the gutter along with two ten dollar bills, but her bus ticket to New Orleans and all the rest of the money was gone.

"What'll I do," Mona cried aloud. She had no money now to get to New Orleans! Tears streamed down her face. Maybe those two women who had helped her up saw the money in the gutter and took it. Or maybe it just blew away. A stiff wind was blowing. All Mona knew was that it was gone.

A man came up to Mona and asked her in Spanish if she was all right. Mona spoke Spanish from taking it in school. Her parents discouraged use of the language. She told the man of her predicament, and he looked sad. He looked very poor. He surely was in no position to loan her money. But he did have a cell phone, and he let Mona use it.

The thought of calling her mother terrified Mona. Mom must totally hate her by now. Mona had run away from home and didn't even leave a note. Mom would never forgive her. She'd probably never allow Mona to return home. She'd call the authorities and have Mona put in a foster home. Mona was shaking so badly that she didn't even know if she could punch in a phone number, even if she knew whom to call.

She thought of Julio Avila then. She'd known him for just a few weeks. They'd had one date, if you could call eating at that little barbeque restaurant a date. Their relationship wasn't deep enough that she could expect Julio to go out of his way to help her. How could she burden the poor guy with her terrible problems when he scarcely knew her?

But Mona didn't know whom else to call. She certainly could not expect Aunt Corinne, who lived on a tight budget, to forward money to a niece when she probably didn't even want Mona to come in the first place.

Mona finally managed to stop shaking enough to punch in the numbers to Julio's cell phone. It was about three thirty in the afternoon on a Monday, and Julio was out of class and walking to his broken-down truck. Mona pictured his phone ringing, and Julio listening to Mona dumping her terrible predicament on his shoulders. Mona would not have blamed him in the least if he said, "Look, you crazy nut, you've caused me enough problems. Your crazy parents are blaming me that you took off. Get lost, babe. I don't even want to hear your name anymore."

"Yeah?" Julio said.

"Julio," Mona sobbed.

"Mona?" he gasped. "Hey, what's up with you, babe? You've got everybody going nuts looking for you." He sounded really concerned. "Are you okay?"

"I'm okay, but I'm in terrible trouble," Mona cried.

"Okay, go slow," Julio said. "Tell me what's going on."

"My mom and I had a terrible fight, and I was so upset I decided to get my savings together and take a bus to New Orleans to stay with my Aunt Corinne, but I fell down getting off this bus, and I wasn't hurt or anything, but my bus ticket and most of my money was lost. I'm standing here on the street with just twenty dollars, and I'm so scared, I don't know what to do," Mona said.

"Where are you?" Julio asked.

"Phoenix," Mona said.

"Arizona? Phoenix, Arizona, whoa!" Julio said.

"Julio, I said mean things to my mom, and she'll hate me forever and never let me come home," Mona said.

"Okay, listen up. Any safe place to eat around there?" Julio asked.

"Yeah, there's a chain restaurant on the corner. And there's a church. I don't know what kind of a church ... oh, wait, it says

Santa Ysabel," Mona said, calming down
a little.

"Okay, good," Julio said after Mona
gave him the street address of the church.
"You get some food, Mona, 'cause you're
probably really hungry, and then you hang
out at the church. I'll come get you, but it's
gonna take like five hours. Let's see, it's
almost four, so look for me around ten, ten
thirty. You tell the padre what's going on,
okay?"

"Oh, Julio, I feel so terrible doing this to
you. I'm so ashamed," Mona cried. "I just
didn't know where else to turn."

"Hey, don't cry, Mona Lisa," Julio said.
"Mona Lisa only smiles, okay? Just hang in
there, babe."

Mona handed the Mexican man back
his cell phone. "*Muchas gracias*," she said.

He smiled and said, "*Por nada*."

Julio Avila drove to the real estate
office where Xavier Corsella worked. His
car was parked outside, so Julio knew he
was in there. Julio ran into the office and

approached Mr. Corsella as he sat at a desk talking to a couple, probably prospects.

"Mr. Corsella, sir," Julio said, bursting into the conversation. "Mona is in Phoenix. She's okay. She wants to come home, and we're going to get her right now, you and me. My old truck isn't reliable so we'll need to use your wheels."

"Thank God she's all right," Mr. Corsella said. "I'll go home and get Martha—"

"We're not picking up your wife, sir," Julio said. "Call her on the way and tell her Mona is okay and that we're bringing her home, but she's not coming with us. The kid is scared out of her mind of that lady."

When they got to the car, Julio said, "Give me the keys, sir. I'm driving. We need to get there as fast as we legally can, and I'm good at stuff like that."

Mr. Corsella nodded and got into the passenger side. He called his wife on his cell phone. "Martha, Mona is all right. She's in Phoenix, and we're going right now to get her. ... What? ... No, dear."

There was a long pause while Mr. Corsella listened to his wife, then he said, "Martha, Julio and I are going to get her. When her back was to the wall, *she didn't call us, Martha.* She called Julio. We've managed to convince our child that we're not on her side. Understand me, Martha. Our little girl is in a strange city, all alone, out of money, desperate, and she called a boy she's known for about ten days, because she thinks he's on her side and we're not. Martha, we should be home in the morning. Julio and I will split the driving." He listened for a few minutes again, and then he said in a weary voice, "Just shut up, Martha, and take a tranquilizer, for crying out loud!"

Julio took the car onto the freeway as he told Mr. Corsella what Mona had told him. "She was fixing to go to New Orleans and try to make a home with this aunt who lives there. She thought she could hang out there until she turned eighteen and could run her own life. Then things kinda went wrong. She lost her bus ticket and her money.

She gave me the address of this church where she's at. I told her to get something to eat and then hang out at the church and tell the padre the story. Mona was crying, like hysterical, but then she calmed down while I talked to her. She's safe there at the church."

"Julio, I cannot tell you how grateful I am that you befriended Mona and gave her a lifeline to hang onto. I shudder to think what might have happened otherwise, I feel so badly about how my wife reacted to you," Mr. Corsella said.

"Well," Julio said, "she's not the first person to be turned off by me and Pop. Let's face it, sir. I'm not every mother's dream of the dude she wants her daughter to hook up with. Me and Pop, we kinda live on the edge. When you talk about the poverty line, we're looking up at it."

Xavier Corsella sighed. "I'm telling you, Julio, I didn't grow up on the right side of the tracks either. I was lucky enough to get a college scholarship and major in economics. I got into the real estate racket, and it was great for a long time. Martha and I both were so busy raking in the money in the housing boom," Mr. Corsella said.

"We have two boys, and we were thinking they'd go to UCLA, maybe Yale, but then the 401(k) bottomed out and the boys joined the Marines for a free education. Martha was talking about getting out of the *barrio*. She's never liked it around here. Anyway, when the real estate market tanked, Martha really went down. She's at the doctor all the time for depression, bad nerves. She can't believe we've slipped so far, and then when Mona started being rebellious." He shook his head sadly.

"Well, Mr. Corsella, there is one good thing about being poor," Julio said. "You never know if the economy is up or down."

"I hear you," Mr. Corsella said. "When Martha and I started dating, we were both in college. She's always wanted Mona to marry well, if you know what I mean."

156

"And then along came Julio Avila," Julio said with a wry smile.

"Julio, I feel so bad about all this," the man said, shaking his head again. "I hang out with Luis Sandoval and Emilio Ibarra. They're regular guys. They're the salt of the earth. Felix Martinez too. They got no problems with a kid like you, or your father for that matter. My mother, may she rest in peace, whenever she'd see a down-and-outer, she'd say, 'There for the grace of God go I.' I could have stood up to Martha and backed Mona. She came to me, almost begging me to stand up for her, and I chickened out. Imagine how I'd feel if she'd run away and come to some harm … I'd never forgive myself."

Xavier Corsella called his wife again as they drove across the desert. "We're making good time, Martha. We passed through Yuma. Julio is an excellent driver. We should get to Phoenix before eleven."

"Oh, Xavier," Martha Corsella groaned, "are you sure Mona is all right? I'm so worried about her. She must be terrified. I cannot believe she did such a thing. I called my sister in New Orleans. Mona didn't even call Corinne and get permission to go there. She was just going to appear on her doorstep. I'm a little bit angry with my sister. She wasn't sympathetic at all. She implied that all of this was my fault, that I'm a bad mother or something. Like she would know when she's a spinster with no children at all! I suppose I shouldn't be surprised. Corinne is such a sad and pathetic person."

"Well, you can talk to Mona when we get to Phoenix, Martha," Mr. Corsella promised. "But you must be kind. She's a fragile young girl. We've got to be careful of what we say."

"Of course, Xavier," Martha Corsella said. "I understand. I'm a mother. A mother knows when to bear down and when to ease up. I'm a mother."

Xavier gave Julio a wry look as they drove on. "She said she's a mother so she won't be harsh on Mona," he said.

158

At ten minutes to eleven, the car pulled into the parking lot of Santa Ysabel Church. A Franciscan sister who looked about thirty came out with Mona. They had apparently been watching from the window, and Mona recognized her father's car.

"There they are, dear," the sister said as the two men got out of the car.

Mona turned and gave the sister a big hug, and then she broke into a run, flying into her father's arms. "Daddy," she screamed. "I'm so sorry. I'm so glad to see you. You don't hate me, do you? Daddy, please forgive me!"

"Hate you, *mi hija*?" Mr. Corsella said. "I love you more than my own life, ten times more. I am so happy to see you. It's the happiest moment of my life!" He kissed his daughter's brow.

Mona turned then and rushed into Julio's arms. "Oh, Julio, you are my knight in shining armor. I wasn't sure if you would help me. I didn't know where to turn, and I wasn't sure you'd help me, but you did! Oh Julio, I think I love you!"

159

Julio put his arms around Mona and hugged her. He took advantage of the opportunity and kissed her on her lips. When he drew back, he glanced at the girl's father, wondering what he was thinking, but Xavier Corsella smiled. Then Julio said to Mona, "Smile on, Mona Lisa."

Mr. Corsella thanked the padre and the sister at the church. Julio saw him giving them a cash donation. The church was very poor, with peeling stucco and many ruts in the blacktop of the parking lot.

"She came to us and said her boyfriend told her to stay with us until he came with her father," the old padre said with a smile. He looked at Julio, at the tall, broad-shouldered boy. "You are the boyfriend, eh?"

"Looks like it, padre," Julio said with a grin.

"Little one," the padre said to Mona, "don't ever run away from home again. And stay close to this *muchacho* because I can see he is a very good boy. He reached in the large pocket of his habit and drew out

160

three rosaries. He gave one to each of them, and then he waved them off.

"I'll take the wheel now, Julio," Mr. Corsella said. He looked at Mona. "Julio drove the whole way here. He thought he could make better time than an old fogey like me, and he was probably right. But it's my turn now. I know a boy like you thinks an older guy can't drive, but you must be exhausted. And I'm not ready for the rocking chair yet."

Julio and Mona got in the backseat, and Julio handed Mona his cell phone. "Your father promised your mother you'd call her when we got here," Julio said. "I think you better take care of it now, babe."

Mona swallowed hard. "I can't. Maybe a little later. But not right now. I mean, she's probably so mad at me that she'll scream and stuff, and I can't take it right now," Mona said.

"Come on, Mona, you gotta. She's sitting there by the phone just waiting to get the call. She won't quite believe you're all right until she hears your voice," Julio said.

Mona's eyes got very large. Her lower lip quivered. "I bet … I bet she totally hates me," Mona whispered in a trembling voice. "I said such mean things to her the last time I saw her, and I ran away and didn't even leave a note."

"Mona," Xavier Corsella said from the front seat, "call your mother. She doesn't hate you. She loves you. Your mother is a very excitable person, and she has bad nerves and depression, but she loves you as much as I do. We would both die for you, Mona. Right after you went away, she rushed down to the church and lit twenty candles for you. I heard her in the bedroom crying and pleading with the Blessed Virgin to bring you home."

"I'm so ashamed of what I did," Mona groaned.

Julio reached over and put his arm around Mona's shoulders, pulling her gently against himself. "Babe, do it. Just punch in those numbers. She's gonna hear the phone ring, and she's gonna grab it and hope with all her heart it's you … go on, babe."

Tears were running down Mona's face as she punched in the numbers to her mother's phone.

The phone had hardly rung before Martha Corsella said, "Yes! Yes?" She sounded like she'd been crying too.

"Mom," Mona said in a small, shaky voice, "I'm so sorry. I'm sorry about the mean things I said and about running away. It was an awful, horrible thing, and I'm so sorry."

"Mona, Mona," Martha Corsella sobbed, "are you all right? Are you sure you're all right? Nothing bad happened to you, did it? Oh, Mona, are you sure you're all right?"

CHAPTER TEN

Yes, Mom, I'm okay. We just left Phoenix. Julio drove all the way to Phoenix, and now Daddy is driving," Mona said.

"Oh, Mona, I prayed so hard. I was so worried," Martha Corsella said.

"We'll be home real early in the morning, Mom. There isn't much traffic, except for big trucks. They're all lit up, and they look like sailing ships going through the darkness," Mona said.

"Have you had something to eat today, Mona?" Mom asked.

"Yeah, I had a big hamburger and fries," Mona said. "Don't worry, Mom. We'll be home before you know it."

"Mona, baby, I love you," Mom said.

"I love you too, Mom," Mona said, beginning to cry again.

Julio put his arm around Mona, and she cuddled up to him, lying back against his shoulder. She was sound asleep in three minutes. Her father looked in the rearview mirror and smiled. "She's out like a light. She's so tired," he said to Julio. Mona was so exhausted that she slept soundly through the soft conversation that took place between her father and Julio during the miles ahead.

"You're quite a runner on the Cougar track team, aren't you, Julio?" Mr. Corsella asked as they ploughed through the darkness across Arizona.

"Yeah, I did really good in the three-mile race in Balboa Park. I'll be going to Fresno now. If I win there, it's huge. My dad is really excited. You should see the guy when I run. Usually he's kinda down because his health isn't too good, you know. His liver is shot, and his heart isn't too good, but when I run, it's like he's ten years younger," Julio said.

"That's great," Mr. Corsella said.

"Yeah. For most of my life, it's been just me and Pop. Mom died when I was real small. I barely remember her. Just this pretty dark lady singing to me, and then she wasn't there anymore. I asked my father where she was, and he said she was singing with the angels. But I was kinda mad at the angels for a while. Losing her was a big blow to my father. He started drinking. Lost his jobs. It's been pretty much all downhill," Julio said.

"Rough," Mr. Corsella said. "I think sometimes it's harder on a man to lose his wife than for a woman to lose her husband. They call women the weaker sex, but I don't buy that for a minute. They're more resilient than we are."

"You know," Julio said in a voice softer than his normal tone, "one thing I remember about Pop. I was maybe eight or something like that. It was getting near to Christmas, he wasn't working as usual, and the holidays were looking pretty lean. Anyway, those

166

do-gooder ladies were having all the needy people come to a parking lot, and they were passing out clothing and food. Pop and I went, and we got a bag of groceries, and then we looked at the clothes. They were giving away these nice fleece coats, real warm. We slept out a lot, and I was so cold. I had my eye on one of those fleece coats. I saw my Pop looking at a fleece jacket too, camel-colored, really warm-looking." Julio sighed.

"Anyway, one of the ladies said there would be just one coat to a family, and there we were, Pop and I, both looking at those fleece jackets. Pop had found a coat in just his size, and he was kinda caressing it. The coat he had, it was no good in the cold. It was an old cloth thing with the lining falling out. Pop wanted that coat, boy, but here I was trying on the coat I'd found, and I was really excited. It was just right for me, but, you know, just one coat to a family. Pop looked at me trying on that warm fleece coat, and he smiled and put the coat he wanted back on the rack. We walked away from there, me in my nice warm fleece coat and him still in that old cloth coat that didn't keep out the chill … didn't do nothing to keep him warm. I felt bad, but boy, I was a kid, an eight-year-old kid, and I wanted that coat so bad, and it felt good. I often think about that day. My pop, he was cold all winter. I'd see him shivering in the cold. He was willing to be cold if his kid could be warm."

Xavier Corsella didn't say anything. He gazed out on the highway, his eyes momentarily turning damp. He thought of the ragged father and the little son in the parking lot where they'd give just one coat to a family. He thought about the father's sacrifice, and here was the boy, remembering it more than ten years later, remembering the sacrifice, his voice heavy with emotion.

"I can tell you love your father a lot, Julio," Mr. Corsella finally said.

"Yeah," Julio said, "I really enjoy

running, but it's as much for him as it is for me, maybe more. I have this dream that I'll get to the Olympics or the world track and field competition one day, or maybe a Boston Marathon, or something. Something big. I want it to blow him away, to put a big smile on his face. It'd be like, you know, the only big, wonderful thing he ever had happen to him."

They passed through Yuma, where the landscape was dotted with the outlines of saguaros, standing like ghostly sentinels in the night. At two in the morning, they crossed the Colorado River.

"Couple more hours," Mr. Corsella said.

Mona was stirring in Julio's arms.

"Maybe we should stop and get something to eat," Julio said.

"Yeah, nice hot coffee and a bacon and egg sandwich would be good," Mr. Corsella said.

The three of them walked into a small diner and ordered coffees and sandwiches.

"I'm getting really nervous," Mona said. "What's Mom *really* thinking?"

"She'll be so happy to see you that she'll forget why she was mad at you," Dad said.

"Tell you what," Julio said. "I'll drive the rest of the way home. I'm all rested now. I'll stop at the real estate office where I left my beater, and then you guys can go home. I don't want to show up at the house and complicate things. At four in the morning, I'm not ready for trouble."

It was quarter to five when Julio pulled the car alongside his rusty pickup. They all got out, and Mr. Corsella gave Julio a hearty handshake.

Then Mr. Corsella grabbed Julio for a hug.

"You're the best," Mr. Corsella said in an emotionally hoarse voice.

Mona went into Julio's arms and clung to him as long as she could. Julio gave Mona a kiss and said he'd see her in school. Then Mona and her father headed home.

Mr. Corsella had called his wife from

the little diner where they had sandwiches and told her they would be home around five. The minute they pulled into the driveway, the front door sprang open, and Martha Corsella came running. She yanked open the door on Mona's side and grabbed her hands, pulling her from the car and kissing her all over her face.

As they headed for the kitchen, Mr. Corsella said, "Martha, Julio is a heckuva boy. If he were my son, I'd be bursting with pride as much as I am with Jimmy and Peter."

Martha Corsella stared at husband, a strange look on her face. Mona could not interpret what was going through her mother's mind. Mona was so grateful to her father for what he said, but she wasn't sure it had resonated with Mom.

In spite of their protestations that they were not hungry after the sandwiches at the diner, Martha Corsella insisted on putting out cookies and more coffee.

Mona had resolved she would never tell

her parents about Tim Kent—how she had been stupid enough to get into a stranger's car—and what could have happened. If she ever relented and *did* tell her parents, it would be at least ten years from now.

Mona insisted on going to school in the morning. She said she had slept a lot on the trip home, and she was not tired. She did not tell her mother about how she had snuggled in Julio's arms all the way home and how that had made her sleep more blissful. Mona did not know, even now, how her mother really felt about Julio Avila.

When Mona's friends, Ernesto, Naomi, Carmen, and Abel, gathered around her at lunch, she told them everything, even the part about Tim Kent. Julio was practicing with Coach Muñoz, so he didn't show up for lunch.

Mona told them all about how she had been stranded in Phoenix and how she was afraid to call her parents, so she called Julio. "I was more scared than I've ever been in my life," she said.

"You could have called us," Ernesto said. "My dad and I would've come for you."

"Or us," Naomi said, although Naomi did not think her father would have been too thrilled about driving to Phoenix in the middle of the night.

"But I was hours and hours away, and it was so awful," Mona said. "I was hoping Julio cared about me enough to come and help me, but I wasn't sure. But he came through like a superhero. He was so wonderful, you guys," Mona said.

"So now your mom isn't down on him anymore, right?" Naomi asked.

"Daddy loves him like a son," Mona said, "but Mom hasn't said anything yet. Dad said some nice things about Julio, but Mom just sorta had a funny look on her face. Mom is real stubborn. When she gets something in her head, it's hard to get it out."

"She'll come around," Carmen said. "What Julio did was just too awesome."

During the afternoon break, Mona went to the vending machines to buy an apple. As she stood there, Julio came walking along. He had a strange look on his face. "How's it going, babe?" he asked. Though he didn't come right out and ask, Mona thought he wanted to know if her mother had accepted him now, even a little.

"Okay, I guess," Mona said. She wanted to tell him that her mother really liked him too how because of what he had done, but she couldn't tell him that because she didn't know. "How about with you, Julio?"

"Uh ... I'm not sure," Julio said. "I got this text message on my phone from, of all people, your mom."

"What?" Mona gasped. "What did she say?"

"It was very brief. She just said, 'Julio, come to dinner at the Corsella home on Cardinal Street at seven tonight. Bring your father too. Martha Corsella.'"

Mona's eyes grew very big. "I can't believe it. She never said anything to me about it. You'd think she would have told me," Mona said.

"So maybe your mom wants to poison me and Pop," Julio said. "A little arsenic in the carne asada."

"Julio!" Mona cried.

"Just joking, babe, but I don't get it," Julio said.

"Maybe she just wants to do something nice for you and your father to thank you for bringing me home. That was a very big deal, you know. You went way out of your way to do that," Mona said.

"Yeah, maybe she wants to say, 'Hey, kid, you did a grand thing, so I made a nice dinner for you as a way to say thank you and good-bye. Oh, and another thing, good riddance,'" Julio said.

"Oh, Julio," Mona wailed. "You're coming, aren't you? I mean, it'd be awful if you didn't come."

"Oh yeah, sure. Me and Pop. I better go home early today and make sure he's sober. He's got to shave, and I'll find some nice clothes for him. Usually Pop wouldn't win any prizes for good dressing. We'll be there, babe. But listen, if your mom disappears into the kitchen and takes a meat cleaver out, warn us. Me and Pop can move fast if necessary. Give us a heads up that we gotta, as Pop says, 'make legs,'" Julio said.

"Julio!" Mona cried again. But in her heart, she was completely mystified. If Mom had softened to Julio, why hadn't she told Mona to ask him to dinner while they were both at school? Maybe, as Julio thought, this was just Mom being polite. She had to thank Julio for what he had done for Mona, but she might also want to make it clear that he was still no more welcome as a boyfriend for her daughter than he was before.

When Mona got home from school, her father wasn't home. He was still showing property to some prospects. But Mom was bustling about the kitchen as she always did when guests were coming. Mom was a very good cook, and she loved trying out new recipes on guests. Mona and her father preferred meat and potatoes without many frills, so the only chance Mom had to show her culinary skills beyond that was when they had company. When the boys were home, they requested carne asada and refried beans almost every day.

"Hi, Mona," her mother said cheerfully. "I bet you had a lot to tell your friends today. I suppose everybody was curious about your … adventure."

"It was interesting, Mom," Mona said nervously. She wasn't sure where her Mom was coming from. She wanted to come right out and ask her mother what was going on with this dinner party tonight, but she was afraid of the answer. She was afraid Mom would put on that stern face and say, "I have good manners, Mona. It is only right that we show our formal appreciation to Julio Avila. And also that we make it clear that we are *not* friends."

"We're having guests over tonight, Mona. Julio has probably already told you.

Him and his father. I thought it was the least we could do to show our gratitude for what he did. Going all that way and back to bring you home. My goodness. Your father tells me the boy is very attached to his father, so we wanted him to come too. He seems like the sort of man who doesn't get to go out to dinner very much."

"That's … nice, Mom," Mona squeaked. She went to her room. She was so afraid of what was about to happen. Mona didn't know how she could put on a happy face all through dinner if it became clear that this was "thank you and good-bye" to Julio and his father.

At quarter to seven, the rusty little pickup appeared, rattling up to the Corsella condo. Mr. Avila looked nice in a rather new sport coat and pressed slacks. He had shaven too, and he was very sober. Julio looked wonderful in a dark sweater and dark jeans. Mona thought he was the most handsome creature on earth.

Xavier Corsella was now home, and he

greeted the Avilas warmly. "Mr. Avila, I got to know your son very well on our long drive to and from Phoenix, and I must say you have a wonderful boy there, and you surely did something right to inspire his respect for you," Mr. Corsella said.

Mr. Avila mumbled, "Thank you," but he seemed very ill at ease.

"Hello, Julio, Mr. Avila," Martha Corsella said. "Dinner is about ready. I hope you like sirloin steak, mashed potatoes with chives, green beans, and lemon chiffon pie."

"Who wouldn't?" Julio said wryly. He couldn't have looked more apprehensively at Mrs. Corsella if she were wearing a long black skirt and a pointy black hat and wielding a broom.

"Oooh, it all looks so good," Mr. Avila smiled with appreciation.

"At home, we rely heavily on those little plastic containers where there are segments of cardboard meat and corn that tastes like yellow peaches," Julio said.

During the meal, the Corsellas talked about the vagaries of the real estate market and how it was picking up just a little. Then Mr. Corsella asked Julio about his triumphs on the track team, and Julio shared them to the delight of his father.

Mona was so nervous she didn't know what she was eating, even though the sirloin steak was so tender it cut like butter, the potatoes were perfectly seasoned, and the green beans were wonderful. When the lemon chiffon pie appeared, it was so beautiful and delicious that it seemed unreal.

Then Martha Corsella said, "There is something I have to say to you, Julio."

Mona felt like she might faint and slide under the table.

"Yes, ma'am," Julio said.

"It's very hard for me to say this, Julio, because I am a very proud woman. No, that's not right: pigheaded is a better way to describe me. I misjudged you. My husband and I are so grateful for how you rescued our little girl above and beyond the call of duty. We are grateful from the bottom of our hearts. But that's not what I really want to say to you, Julio. *This is what I must say.* When you come to pick up Mona to take her out, please come in the house. We will always be glad to see you. And, Mr. Avila, let me say this … you have every right to be proud of such a son as Julio. I have known many young men, including my own two sons, but I have never known a finer one than your son."

Mona closed her eyes against the tears that flowed freely, but her lips were smiling with a smile that would have done Mona Lisa proud. Martha Corsella had learned a powerful lesson and had admitted she was wrong. She had deeply misjudged Julio and his father based on their circumstances and social status. But she learned that character comes first.

ANNE SCHRAFF

URBAN UNDERGROUND

MISJUDGED

"He's in one of my classes. Can we just change the subject? It doesn't mean anything. Can we just drop it?"

Mona Lisa is average in the looks department. Or so she thinks. Zero self-confidence. Insecure. She's never dated. That is, until Julio Avila, star of the Chavez track team, asks her out. But her uppity mother has other ideas. The Avilas are not the "right sort of people." And mother knows best.

SADDLEBACK
PUBLISHING
www.sdlback.com

ISBN: 978-1-62250-764-1

9 781622 507641

90000